HEY, DAD, GET A LIFE!

TODD STRASSER

HEY, DAD, GET A LIFE!

Published by Troll Communications L.L.C.

Published by arrangement with Holiday House, Inc., New York.

First paperback edition published 1998.

Printed in the United States of America.

10 9 8 7 6 5 4 3 2 1

Library of Congress Cataloging-in-Publication Data
Strasser, Todd.
    Hey, Dad, get a life / Todd Strasser. — 1st ed.
        p.   cm.
    Summary: When a supernatural presence begins doing favors for Kelly and her younger sister, Sasha, they realize that the ghost of their dead father has returned to watch over them.
        ISBN 0-8234-1278-4 (lib. bdg.)   ISBN 0-8167-4530-7 (pbk.)
    [1. Ghosts — Fiction.   2. Fathers and daughters — Fiction.
3. Sisters — Fiction.]   I. Title.
PZ7.S899He   1996   96-46839   CIP   AC
[Fic] — dc21

In Memory of Lenore Epstein Older

I am grateful to a young lady named Elena Tonasino, who appeared one morning through the curtains on the stage at the Garden City Middle School, where I was speaking. By generously sharing the tragic details of her father's unexpected death, she helped give this book life.

HEY, DAD, GET A
LIFE!

1

"Why are we having science?" my little sister, Sasha, asked. "I thought we had that in school."

"Not science," I said. "A *séance*."

We were sitting in the tree house Dad built for us the summer before last. I shivered a little. It was cold and almost dark, and I was wearing a hooded sweatshirt.

Sasha was wearing her denim jacket with the red plaid lining. She was eight. Sitting on the floor of the tree house with her knees pulled under her chin, she chewed on a strand of her long black hair.

I had just turned twelve. My hair was also black, but it was full of annoying waves so I wore it short and pulled the bangs away from my face with barrettes.

On the floor between us was a coffee can. Inside, a white candle flickered, filling the tree house with the faintest light. We weren't supposed to fool around with fire, especially when Mom wasn't there, but I'd decided to make an exception just this once.

Sasha screwed up her face. "What's a séance?"

"It's when we mortals get in touch with the hereafter."

"The hereafter what?"

"It's just the hereafter," I said. "It's where our spirits go after we die."

"I thought they went to heaven or hell."

"They're both part of the hereafter, I think."

"How come I never heard of it before?" my sister asked.

"You don't learn about it until middle school," I said, getting a little tired of her questions. "Now we have to hold hands and close our eyes and really concentrate."

"On what?" Sasha asked.

"On making Dad appear."

Sasha's eyes widened. "He can *do* that?"

Sometimes she could really drive me crazy. "How would I know? *You're* the one who thinks he's a ghost. I'm just trying to help. Now hold my hand and close your eyes and let's concentrate on seeing Dad's ghost before Mom gets home and has a fit."

Sasha placed her hands in mine, and we closed our eyes. Personally, I didn't believe in ghosts. The only reason I'd decided to have the séance was to prove to Sasha that it was all in her head. But now, sitting on the cold wooden floor of the tree house, I found myself praying that I was wrong.

"Try to picture Dad," I said.

"Where?"

"Over the candle flame."

"Is he big or little?"

"Medium."

"What's he wearing?"

"Give me a break, Sasha. How am I supposed to know?"

"I mean, is he wearing a sheet? Is he all white like Casper or greenish like one of those mean ghosts?"

"Dad wouldn't be a mean ghost."

"Okay, I'm going to picture a medium-size white ghost," she said.

"Good idea."

"What are you picturing?"

"The same thing. Now be quiet. Ghosts don't come if you're talking."

Sasha was quiet for about a millisecond. "Kel?"

"Now what?"

"You don't think he grew a beard in the hereafter, do you?"

"I really don't think it matters," I said. "Just be quiet!"

"You don't have to get all huffy," Sasha said.

"Look, do you want to see Dad or not?" I asked impatiently.

"Sure, I want to see him," she said. "I just don't want to imagine him wrong."

"If he shows up, he'll look however he wants," I said. "Now, for the last time, be quiet and concentrate."

I squeezed my sister's hand in mine and imagined Dad in his denim shirt, cowboy boots, and jeans. I could picture him in so many places in those clothes: on the sideline at a soccer game, in the audience during a school play, driving me and my friends to the movies on a rainy Saturday afternoon, waiting in the pet store while Sasha and I looked at all the animals Mom wouldn't let us get.

That was the thing about Dad.

He'd always been there.

I missed him so much. It was like an ache deep inside that would never, ever go away.

Oh, please, I found myself wishing, *why can't he be a ghost?*

2

"Girls? Are you out here?" It was Mom, calling through the dark to us from the kitchen door.

From the tree house I yelled back, "Yeah, we're here."

"Time for dinner," Mom called.

In the flickering candlelight, I looked at my sister. "Any sign of him?"

Sasha shook her head. Not that I'd expected anything; I was too old to believe in ghosts. Just the same, deep inside I felt a bitter wave of disappointment.

Sasha started to climb down the wooden steps Dad had nailed to the tree trunk. I bent over the can and blew out the flame, then followed her.

But halfway down I felt an odd sensation and looked back up at the tree house.

A faint light glowed between the wooden planks.

"Kel?" Sasha said from the ground below.

"Yeah?" I looked down.

"You coming?"

"Just a sec." I looked up again. The tree house was dark. It must have been my imagination.

"What were you two doing in the tree house?" Mom asked when we came into the kitchen. She was wearing her business clothes — a white blouse and a navy blue skirt. She worked in town as a paralegal and rarely got home before seven o'clock.

"Just playing," I answered. Three glasses were stacked in the middle of the kitchen table, along with some silverware and napkins. The place mats were still there from breakfast. A dried Cheerio was stuck to mine.

The microwave on the kitchen counter hummed. Mom gazed out the kitchen window into the dark. In the past year she'd gotten more wrinkles around her eyes and more gray in her long black hair. She was the only mom I knew who had really long hair. She always wore it in a ponytail.

Bing! The microwave bell rang; dinner was ready. Mom was still staring outside.

"Mom?" I said. "You okay?"

She took a deep breath and seemed to tremble a little. With the tip of her finger, she rubbed something out of the corner of her eye. "It's been a long time since you played in there."

Sasha and I shared a quick, nervous glance. We hadn't been in the tree house since Dad died.

"Could you do me a favor, kids?" Mom asked, opening the microwave and taking out three steaming dinners on plastic trays.

"Sure, anything," I said.

"Don't play in the tree house just yet," she said.

3

It's the night Dad went away for the last time. He and I are standing by the front door. I slide my arms around him and hug, pressing the side of my face against his chest. A button from his tan coat presses against my cheek. "Do you have to go?"

"You know I do, hon."

"What if something bad happens?" I hug as hard as I can. His briefcase is on the floor. It's made of hand-tooled leather and smells like a saddle.

"Nothing bad is going to happen," he assures me.

"Promise?"

He puts his arms around me and gives me a big hug.

"Hon?" Mom's voice brought me back. She and Sasha were standing in the doorway of my bedroom, Sasha in pink pajamas, Mom still in her business clothes. Loose strands of black hair hung around her face.

"This room's a complete disaster." Mom sounded tired.

I was sitting on my bed, surrounded by schoolbooks and papers. I was in the middle of math homework. "I'll straighten up in the morning."

"Look at Sasha's room," Mom said. "It's spotless and she's only eight."

"She's also a slug," I muttered.

"Mom!" Sasha gasped. "Is that a bad word?"

"Well, not exactly," Mom said. "But it's not a good word, either."

"Then you're a big slug," Sasha shot back.

I put my hand over my heart. "I'm mortally wounded."

"How's your homework?" Mom asked.

"Almost done." Math made me think of Dad because he used to help me. Sometimes I thought about asking Mom for help, but she was always so tired at night. Besides, math wasn't her strong suit.

"I'm going to read to Sasha," she said with a yawn.

After they left, I looked around my room. Copies of *Seventeen* and *Mad* magazines and my black backpack were lying on the floor. Sample sheets of wallpaper for my dollhouse were scattered here and there. Shirts, sweaters, and jeans hung over the brass rail at the foot of my bed. Dad had found the rail in someone's garbage. He'd fixed it, polished it, and bolted it to the frame of my bed.

I looked back down at my math. It was so boring. I decided to finish it the next morning.

After putting on my pajamas, I went into Sasha's room to listen to Mom read. Sasha's room was the only neat place in the house. Until a few weeks before, it had been a worse pig sty than mine. Then Mom started the star chart. Any day that we managed to straighten our rooms and make our beds before we left for school, we got a star. Once we earned twenty stars, we could get something little, like a book or a pack of stickers. Forty stars earned a small toy or a CD, and seventy-five stars would get you a nice doll or stuffed animal.

Sasha had her heart set on Andy Panda, a huge stuffed black-and-white panda that sat in the window of Miller's Toy Store. Mom said that Andy was in a special category. To get him, Sasha was going to have to earn 200 stars.

Currently, she had eleven stars compared to my two.

I sat in the chair by Sasha's desk. Mom was sitting on the edge of my sister's bed. She read:

"Are you really a ghost?" Freddy asked.

"Yes," replied the ghostly white form.

"Why are you here?" asked Freddy.

"This is where I've always lived," answered the ghost.

A few weeks before, when Sasha first asked Mom to read ghost stories, it seemed creepy. I still felt nervous at night without Dad in the house. Every strange rattle and thump in the dark scared me. I couldn't understand why Sasha would want to hear stories about ghosts.

But still, I listened almost every night.

Mom continued to read:

The ghost floated up in the air, winked at Freddy, then disappeared straight through the wall, never to be seen again.

She closed the book. "The end."

Sasha was sitting up in bed, hugging Puffy, a big old stuffed brown bear that she'd dressed in a blue-and-yellow soccer jersey. "One more page?"

Mom rubbed her temples with her fingers. "I'm sorry, hon. I've got another one of those headaches. We'll start the next story tomorrow night."

"Dad always read more," Sasha said.

"Give her a break," I said. "Didn't you hear her say she had a headache?"

My sister lowered her gaze. "Sorry, Mom."

Mom sighed and opened the book again. "Okay, one more page."

"Oh, good." Sasha smiled. In some ways she was a smart little kid; in other ways she was still too young to understand.

Mom read the first page of a new ghost story, then kissed Sasha on the forehead. She stood up. "Time to sleep."

Sasha slid down until the covers touched her chin. "Mom?"

"Yes, hon?"

"Do you believe in ghosts?"

Mom stopped near the door. "No."

"Then why do they write stories about them?"

"They write stories about lots of things that aren't true," Mom said. "That's why writers have imaginations."

"I believe in them," Sasha said. "I think *we* have a ghost."

Mom yawned. You could see that she had other things on her mind. Probably a long list of stuff she still had to do before she could go to bed.

"Just tell it not to make a mess," she said.

"It's a *he*," said Sasha.

Mom nodded and yawned again. "Come on, Kel. It's time for your sister to go to sleep."

As I left Sasha's room, I wondered why she still insisted there was a ghost after our failed séance. Oh, well, she was a little kid, and little kids can believe whatever they want.

4

"Kelly!" Coach Bosky cupped his hands around his mouth and shouted across the soccer field at me.

I was in the sweeper position, the last line of defense before the goalie. At that moment, two girls from the Tigers were dribbling the ball past me.

I'd been daydreaming, squinting off under the brilliant sunlight at the trees that lined the field. It was a bright, sunny day in early October. The sky was deep blue and the sun seemed stronger than usual.

"Go, Kelly!" Coach Bosky shouted.

I started to run, angry at myself for not paying attention. Sometimes being a defender was boring. If the ball was down at the other end of the field, there was nothing to do except gaze off at the clouds or study the blades of grass at my feet or daydream.

In the old days, I'd had a secret weapon: Dad. He was always there on the sidelines in his blue jeans, denim shirt, and cowboy boots. If the other team started to move the ball toward our goal, he'd yell, "On your toes, Kel!"

The two girls from the Tigers had gotten past me. Now the only one who could stop them from scoring was Emily, our goalie and my best friend. She crouched in front of the goal, her blond hair pulled back into a ponytail and her green-and-blue goalie's jersey flapping slightly in the breeze. Her hands, in the red-and-yellow goalie gloves, were spread. Suddenly she charged the girl with the ball.

Just then the girl passed it to her teammate.

Now the other girl had the ball right in front of the goal. It was a wide open shot, impossible to miss.

And it was all my fault.

As I watched helplessly, I thought, *If only you were here, Dad. If only you'd warned me!*

The girl from the Tigers kicked. But instead of sailing into the goal, the ball spun off the side of her shoe and rolled right to Emily.

She reached down and picked it up.

Everything stopped.

For a moment there was nothing but silence on the field.

No one moved or spoke. We just stood there as if we couldn't believe what we'd seen. Emily stared down at the ball in her hands with a look of total disbelief.

Tweet! Tweet! Tweet! The ref's whistle blew, the game was over. A cheer rose up from our side of the field. Emily and I looked at each other with our mouths open.

"We won!" She dropped the ball and we hugged. A second later we were surrounded by the other members of our team, the Leopards.

"Can you believe it?" Everyone was yelling and hugging one another. "Can you believe she missed?"

Out of the corner of my eye I saw the girl from the Tigers press her face into her hands and cry. Two other players from her team patted her sympathetically on the shoulder.

We crowded around boxes of doughnut holes and jugs of Gatorade for our victory meal. Our parents stood nearby, glowing with pride. Mom wasn't there because she always took Sasha to ballet on Saturdays. Mr. Davis, Emily's dad, was telling anyone who'd listen how his daughter had "saved" the game. He was a heavy, red-faced man with a loud voice. I watched as he cornered Coach Bosky.

"Pretty good for a kid who never played goalie before, huh, Coach?" Mr. Davis said proudly.

Coach Bosky nodded. He was a tall, thin white-haired man with bushy eyebrows. He was wearing green shorts and a white sweatshirt.

"It's the extra practice she's getting," Mr. Davis

went on. "After I get home from work we go out and I kick balls at her."

Coach Bosky looked as if he was only half-listening. His gaze settled on me. "Kelly, can I speak to you for a moment?"

"Yes, Coach?" Biting my lip nervously, I followed him a short distance away.

He crossed his arms and spoke softly so no one else could hear. "You okay?"

I wasn't really sure what he meant. Sometimes it seemed that when people asked that, they were really asking about Dad. "Except for what just happened."

"We were lucky," Coach Bosky said.

"I know." I felt my face flush with embarrassment.

"Next Saturday we've really got to stay in focus."

"Definitely."

Coach Bosky smiled. "A miracle like that comes only once in a lifetime."

I had no reason to doubt him.

5

At school on Monday morning, Emily and I walked to math together. We were sixth-graders at the Franklin Middle School, an old three-story brick building that was always either too hot or too cold.

The hall was crowded with kids wearing backpacks. Ahead of us a group of popular boys and girls were hanging around outside the math room, waiting for the bell to ring before they went in. Emily and I squeezed past them. We weren't unpopular, but we weren't popular, either.

It wasn't that the popular girls were prettier than we were.

The problem was something else.

We were too tall. Especially Emily.

If you looked at the most popular girls in our grade, they had certain things in common. They were attractive; they were smart; they were athletic, but not *too* athletic; and they were usually about the same height as the popular boys.

Emily and I were at a genetic disadvantage, and there was nothing we could do about it.

"Hey, Kel." Inside the classroom Scott Shore came up to me. Scott had short brown hair and the smallest ears I'd ever seen. He was a friendly boy, but the top of his head came up to my nose. Scott liked me. In fifth grade, he'd always wanted to be my partner at dance class on Friday nights.

"Oh, hi, Scott," I said.

Scott glanced at Emily and then back at me. "Uh, could I talk to you alone?"

"See ya in a sec." Emily winked and went to her desk.

"So, uh, did you ask your mom?" Scott asked in a low voice when we were alone.

"She said I can't," I said.

Scott's face fell. "How come?"

"I'm too young."

"It's no big deal," he said. "Just for pizza after school."

"I know, but that's what she said." I'd liked Scott the year before, mostly because he was the first boy ever to like *me*. But now I wasn't so sure.

"What if I get someone to ask Emily, and the four of us go?" Scott said. "Would that be okay?"

"Maybe," I said. "I'll have to ask."

"Okay. I'll try to find someone," Scott said. "Talk to you later." He went to his desk and I went to mine, which was right in front of Emily's. We sat by the windows where the sun streamed in, warming us in the winter and making us too hot in the late spring.

In a low voice I told Emily what Scott had proposed.

"I hope he finds someone who comes up past my chin," she whispered back. "You study for the math quiz?"

"Sort of," I replied, rolling my eyes.

"I know what you mean," Emily said. "It's totally boring."

"And Ratsky's no picnic, either," I said.

Emily chuckled. Ratsky's name was really Mr. Rasky. He was our math teacher, and he had a big nose with little black hairs growing out of it. If you closed your eyes and pretended, you could imagine it being a rat's nose, and the little black hairs being whiskers. And he had a personality to match.

The bell rang and Ratsky came into the room.

"All right, ladies and gentlemen, take your seats," he said as he went up and down the aisles handing out test sheets. "No talking. You'll have twenty minutes, beginning now."

I looked down at the sheet and knew I should have

studied more. The problems were really hard and I felt a sick sensation in my stomach. There was a good chance I was going to fail.

Oh, Dad, I wish you were still here, I thought. *You would have made me study harder. You would have helped me understand this.*

6

I was supposed to go straight home every day after school so that I could be there when Sasha got home. But that day Ms. Keller, my history teacher, made me stay after to finish a history project.

When I finally got home, my sister's backpack was lying inside the front door.

"Sasha?" I called.

She didn't answer. I went into the kitchen. All the lights were on and a bowl with a spoon in it was sitting on the table. An open box of Kix stood near the bowl, so I knew she'd had a snack.

I checked the den, but the TV was off.

"Sasha?" I went upstairs and looked in her room, but she wasn't there. Next I tried Mom's bedroom. The bed was unmade and her bathrobe was lying on the floor. A black skirt and a pink blouse were draped over the chair. All the lights were on. The door to

Dad's closet was slightly ajar, open just enough to let in a little light.

I opened the closet door. Sasha was sitting on the floor, her knees tucked up to her chin, holding Dad's leather wallet close to her nose.

She looked up at me, her skin ghostly pale in the dim light. "Where were you?"

"Dumb Ms. Keller kept me after school," I said.

"I was scared," said Sasha.

This wasn't the first time I'd found her in Dad's closet. "Want to watch some TV?" I asked.

Sasha started to get up, still clutching the wallet. "He's in here, you know."

"Come off it, Sasha."

"I'm serious."

"Then why didn't he come to the séance?" I asked.

"I don't know, but he's here."

I looked around. The closet was almost empty. Mom had given away most of Dad's clothes, but a few things remained — a pair of faded blue jeans, scuffed brown cowboy boots, and his leather brief-case.

"Where?" I asked.

"You can't see him," she said.

"Can you?"

"No."

"Then how do you know?" I asked.

"I just do."

Are all little sisters this weird? I wondered.

"When are you going to teach me to ride a bike?" Sasha asked Mom that night at dinner. We were sitting in the kitchen.

"This weekend, hon."

"That's what you say *every* week."

"Maybe Kelly could teach you," Mom said.

"No way." Sasha shook her head. "She'd let me fall."

"Would you do that?" Mom asked me.

"Better believe it." I nodded.

Mom gave me an exasperated look but didn't say anything. I listened to the *plink . . . plink* of the faucet as it dripped over the dirty dishes in the sink. It had been dripping for months—something Dad would have fixed long ago.

"Kids, I have to tell you something." Mom sounded serious. I braced myself for bad news.

She got fired.

We're going to have to move.

She has cancer and is going to die.

"I'm having dinner with someone tomorrow night," she said. "Kristen's going to sit."

Sasha and I traded a look. We were both thinking, *What's the big deal?*

"He's a friend of Jeannette's," Mom added.

Jeannette Garvey had red hair and was divorced and lived across the street. She was Mom's best friend and was always telling her to go out and have fun.

"So?" Sasha said.

"I thought you should know," Mom said. "He's divorced and has a boy and a girl almost the same ages as you."

Sasha and I shared another puzzled look.

"We already have friends," my sister said.

"That's not why we're getting together."

"Then why?" Sasha asked.

"Well, why do men and women go out to dinner?" Mom asked back.

"Because they're hungry?" Sasha guessed.

Mom smiled a little. "Why else?"

"Ohmygosh!" I stared at her, stunned. "It's a *date*?"

Mom nodded.

Sasha's eyes grew big. "What about . . . ?"

"Dad?" Mom finished the question for her, then looked down at her half-finished microwave French bread pizza.

Plink . . . plink. The faucet dripped.

"I still love your father very much," Mom said.

"Then how can you —" I started to ask.

"It's hard to live alone," Mom said haltingly. "I miss the companionship."

"You have friends," I said.

"It's not the same," said Mom.

"Are you going to get married?" Sasha asked.

"It's just for dinner," Mom said. "I'll be home by nine and I expect both of you to be washed and in bed."

Plink . . . plink.

"Do you have to *kiss* him?" Sasha asked.

"Not unless I want to," Mom answered.

7

"Mom's got a date tonight," I told Emily the next morning as we walked down the hall to math.

Emily wrinkled her nose. "Why?"

"She says she needs companionship."

"Maybe she'd like Anna. My mom's always complaining about how much she sheds."

"She says a dog is too much work," I said. "The thing is, she can't get married until I go to college. I can't be here when he moves in."

"Yuck." Emily winced at the thought. "Triple gross."

We went into Ratsky's classroom and sat at our desks.

Emily gave me a dismal look. "Ready?"

"For?" I asked.

"We get back the quiz, remember?"

I felt my spirits sink. I'd never failed a math quiz in my life. This was going to be a first.

A few moments later Ratsky came into the room. He opened his briefcase and started handing back the quizzes.

"Good work, Kelly," he said, as he gave me my quiz. I thought he was being sarcastic. Then I looked down and saw a big red 100% at the top of the page!

I felt my eyes bug out. Every answer was filled in! And they were all correct!

It wasn't possible.

I'd left nine answers blank.

"I thought you bombed," Emily whispered, looking over my shoulder.

"I — I thought I did," I stammered.

"You call that bombing?"

"Come on, genius," Emily said when class ended.

"Go ahead," I said. "I want to talk to Ratsky."

Emily went to her next class. Ratsky was in the front of the room, erasing the blackboard. I waited until the classroom was empty.

"Excellent job, Kelly," Ratsky said when he noticed me.

"Uh, thanks, Mr. Rasky, but I sort of need to talk to you about it," I said.

"Something wrong?" Ratsky dusted off his hands and sat down at his desk.

"I'm not sure," I said.

Ratsky gave me a quizzical look. I decided to simply tell him the truth.

"When I handed in the quiz yesterday, I left nine answers blank. And I'm pretty sure that even some of the ones I answered were wrong."

Ratsky frowned.

"Someone must have filled in the answers for me," I said.

"I don't see how," he said. "I put the quizzes in my briefcase so I wouldn't forget to take them home. They didn't come out again until I graded them last night."

"Then someone went into your briefcase during school," I said.

The lines in Ratsky's forehead deepened. "It stays in the closet and I lock the door when I leave the room. Let me see the quiz."

I showed it to him.

"That's your handwriting, isn't it?" he asked.

"Well . . ." I hesitated. It couldn't have been, and yet the handwriting on the problems I didn't answer was *exactly* the same as on the problems I did answer.

"It looks like the same pencil to me, and look." Ratsky pointed to the work space at the bottom of the quiz. "There's all your work. I don't see how you can say you didn't do it, Kelly."

Ratsky handed back the quiz. I didn't know what to say. But something very strange had happened.

8

The next few periods passed in a fog. I felt weird and off balance. Nothing could explain how those quiz answers had gotten there.

"Mars to Kelly." Emily was sitting across from me at lunch with a funny look on her face.

"Huh?"

She gestured over her right shoulder. Scott was coming toward us with a boy we didn't know. He must have been new at school. He had brown hair that was a little long, a nice smile, clear blue eyes, and thick eyebrows. But he was no taller than Scott.

"Anyone sitting here?" Scott asked.

"Have a seat," I said.

Scott and the new boy put their trays on the table and sat down. "Turner Gebhart, meet Kelly Halkit and Emily Davis."

"Hi." Turner smiled at us. Some boys got nervous and silly around girls, but he seemed calm and relaxed.

"Turner's from Kansas," Scott said. "He just moved here."

"How come you moved now?" I asked. "School started almost two months ago."

"My mom changed jobs," Turner said.

"Your *mom*?" Emily scowled. "What about your dad?"

"He and my mom split up a couple of years ago," Turner said.

"Guess who his mom is?" Scott said.

"Uh, *Mrs*. Gebhart?" I guessed.

Turner grinned.

"She's someone you've heard of," Scott said. "I'll give you a hint — TV."

Emily's eyes widened. "Is she an actress or something?"

"Not really," Turner said, then took a bite out of his burger.

"Is she *on* TV or *in* TV?" I asked.

"Oh, she's definitely *on* it," said Scott.

"So we'd see her?"

"Every night," Scott said with a smile.

Nobody was on *every night* except the talk show hosts and . . . newscasters.

"The news?" I guessed.

Scott nodded. Meanwhile, Turner quietly ate his lunch.

"Which one?" Emily asked.

Scott's smile grew broader. "Karen Gebhart, the new health and science editor on Channel Eight."

"I've heard of her!" Emily gasped and looked at Turner. "That's so cool! Could we see her tonight?"

Turner bobbed his head up and down.

"Awesome!" Emily said.

Scott looked at me. "So, what do you think, Kel? Want to go for pizza *now*?"

9

That night I ate dinner in the den and watched the six o'clock news on Channel Eight. Mom was off on her "date," and Kristen Yormak was baby-sitting.

Kristen was only two years older than me. She was sort of chubby and had straight brown hair that she parted in the middle. She always arrived at our house with her backpack full of books. As soon as Mom left, Kristen would sit down on the living room couch and do her homework. Sasha and I could have burned down the house and she probably wouldn't have noticed. At exactly eight-thirty, she would look up from her books and say, "Go to bed, girls." That was practically the only time we ever heard her speak.

"You're not supposed to eat in here." Sasha stood in the den doorway.

"Bug off," I said and continued to eat and watch.

"Than I can eat in here, too," she said.

"Suit yourself."

Sasha went into the kitchen and came back with a mircowaved mini-pizza. She sat down on the floor in front of the TV. "Why are we watching the news?"

"There's someone I have to see," I said.

It took a while before Karen Gebhart appeared on the screen. She had brown hair like Turner's and the same blue eyes and thick eyebrows.

Brrriiiinnnng! The phone rang.

"Definitely," I said when I answered it.

"Isn't that cool?" Emily asked, not surprised that I knew she was calling. "He's famous!"

"Well, I don't know, Em. Maybe his mom is."

"Same difference. Come on, Kel, we *have* to go for pizza with them."

"I still have to ask my mom," I said.

"Don't *ask* her, *tell* her."

"Sure, Em." I got off the phone. Talking about going out, I wondered what Mom was doing with Jason whoever he was. What if he was good-looking and nice and Mom fell in love with him? What if at that very moment they were sitting at a candlelit table in the corner of some quiet dark restaurant, talking in low voices and making gooey eyes at each other.

Eeeeeeewwww! Yucko! The thought sent a shiver through me. It wasn't right. It wasn't fair to Dad . . .

or to me. Mom shouldn't be doing this now. She had to wait until I was in college and out of the house. What if she brought the guy home to meet us? I'd die!

Oh, Dad, I wish you were still here. I wish you'd go into that restaurant and dump a pitcher of ice water on his head.

"Would you read to me?" Sasha was standing at my doorway in her pajamas. I was sitting on my bed, doing homework.

"Give me a break," I groaned.

"Please?"

"Oh, okay." I sighed and reluctantly went into her room. Sasha got under the covers with Puffy.

I picked up the book of ghost stories and sat down on the side of Sasha's bed, just like Mom always did.

"One page," I said.

"Come on, even Mom reads more than that," said Sasha.

"Okay, *two* pages."

I wound up reading a whole story.

"Thanks," Sasha said when I was finished.

"You're not welcome."

"Why are you so mean to me?"

I looked down at her, nestled under the covers and hugging Puffy. Big brown eyes, pale skin, and all that black hair. She was right. I was being mean to her. And she was only a little kid.

"I guess I'm just mad because Mom's out with that guy."

"Think they'll get married?"

"I don't know. I hope not. I'll run away if they do."

"Me too." My sister reached under her pillow and took out Dad's old wallet. She slept with it every night. She opened it and took out his driver's license with the little picture of him. He was wearing a blue denim shirt with a white T-shirt under it. The lights from the camera reflected off his shiny forehead. He was shorter than other dads and a little chubby and his hair had receded most of the way back, leaving the top of his head bare. He wore what was left in a little ponytail. Sasha and I used to tease him about it, but he'd only smile. It was almost impossible for him to get angry at us.

I felt tears begin to well up in my eyes. I gritted my teeth and blinked them back. No, I wouldn't cry. I had to be strong like Mom.

"Why does Mom have to go out?" Sasha asked.

"You heard her," I said. "She gets lonely."

"She has us," Sasha said. Then, as an afterthought, she added, "and her friends."

I pictured Turner with his easygoing smile and blue eyes. "It's not the same thing." I actually bent over and kissed her on the forehead, like Mom did. "G'night, Sasha."

"G'night, Kel."

I left her room and went into mine.

It wasn't until I got into bed that I thought again about the math quiz. I'd tried to avoid thinking about it all night. Something really strange and truly inexplicable had happened. It made me feel weird and uncertain.

But what could I do about it?

10

"Oh, Lord! Everyone up!" Mom called out the next morning. "Sasha, Kel! We're late!"

I rubbed my eyes, sat up in bed, and looked at the clock. We'd overslept. Unless we hurried we were going to miss the schoolbus.

I got dressed and went down to the kitchen. Mom was wearing her old white bathrobe with the faint pink stain from the time I tried to do the laundry and mixed up the colors. She was fumbling around with her coffee. The kitchen table was bare.

I opened a cabinet and got out a bowl. "How'd it go last night?"

"Don't ask." She was always short on words until her second cup of coffee.

"He was a real jerk?" I asked hopefully.

"Who knows?"

"Huh?"

"I'll tell you later. I've got to get dressed." She took her coffee and left the kitchen.

I was finishing my cereal when Sasha straggled in. Her hair was its typical morning rat's nest.

"Tie my shoe?" She sat down and held her foot up to me.

"Tie it yourself," I said.

"It takes too long when I do it," she whined.

"Tough."

"Dad always tied *your* shoes," Sasha said.

"Just my soccer cleats," I said. "That was different."

"No, it's not."

"You'd better eat or you're going to miss breakfast," I said.

"I can't eat until my shoes are tied." Sasha crossed her arms and refused to budge. At times like that I wanted to kill her.

Instead, I tied her shoes.

"You're never going to have time to make your bed," I said. "No star for you this morning."

"Want to bet?" Sasha asked as she got a bowl out of the cabinet.

"Sure."

"The dishes."

"Deal." The kitchen sink probably contained three day's worth of dishes. Nothing would make me happier than seeing her wash them all that night.

* * *

I had just finished making my bed when I heard Sasha come upstairs and go into her room. By now Mom was back downstairs.

"Come on, kids," she called from the front hall. "You're going to miss the — Oh, darn! There it goes. Now I have to drive you. Let's go or I'll be late for work. Sasha!"

"Coming!" Sasha called from her room. Her door was closed. Inside I heard her say, "Oh, I wish you'd straighten my room for me. *Please!*"

Fat chance, I thought with a smile. *Prayers aren't going to work today.*

"Come on, kids!" Mom called again.

I headed down the stairs. A moment later Sasha followed. She couldn't have had time to make her bed.

We went down the front steps. Sasha and I called our car the Dirtmobile. Someone had rubbed the words, "Wash Me" into the dirt on the side.

"Well, they're right," Mom admitted as we got in. "I have to get this thing washed one of these days."

"And change the oil," I reminded her. "Dad used to do it every four months or three thousand miles. Whichever came first."

"Right," Mom said in a tone that implied she'd probably never get around to it even though she knew she should. "Seat belts, everyone." She turned to me. "Bed made?"

"Yup." I smiled proudly.

Mom looked in the rearview mirror. "How about you, Sasha?"

"Yup." Sasha imitated me.

I turned and looked over the seat at her. "No way. You didn't have time."

"Did too."

She had to be lying. It would have been impossible for her to make her bed that fast. Mom started to pull the Dirtmobile out of the driveway. Bright red flashes of the morning sun glinted through the tree branches.

Suddenly I had the strangest feeling. "Wait!"

Mom hit the brake. "What?"

"I, uh . . . forgot something," I said, pushing open the car door. "Be right back."

"But —" Before Mom could stop me, I jumped out of the car and rushed back up the front steps. I let myself into the house, quickly climbed the stairs, and pushed open the door to Sasha's room.

Her bed was made. The corners were perfect, and the blanket and top sheet were turned down. The pillow was puffed up and smooth. Her pajamas were neatly folded on the rail and all her stuffed animals were lined up.

The room was perfect!

11

Beep! Beep! Mom honked the car horn impatiently.

I took one last look at Sasha's room. Even the window shades were level.

Beep! Beep!

I hurried downstairs and out to the car, and jumped into the back with Sasha.

"Finally." Mom pulled the Dirtmobile out of the driveway and drove quickly down the street.

In the backseat, I locked eyes with my sister.

"How did you do it?" I whispered.

Sasha stared out the window, ignoring me. She knew something. Whatever it was, I was going to find out.

Mom dropped Sasha off at the elementary school. I watched her hurry toward the front doors.

The filled-in answers on my math quiz . . .

The magically made bed . . .

What's going on?

"Still wondering about last night?" Mom asked as she drove me to the middle school.

"Oh, uh . . . yeah." I'd completely forgotten.

"What a disaster," Mom said. "I got out of work and one of the tires was flat. It took forever to get it changed, and then I couldn't find the directions to the restaurant. I *know* I put them in my bag, but they just disappeared. I called Jason at La Reserve to tell him I'd be late, but by then we'd lost our reservation. We agreed to meet at the Elmsford Diner, but he never showed up. Finally he called and said *his* car battery had died. A comedy of errors."

"So you never got to have dinner with him?" I asked.

Mom shook her head.

The eerie memory of Sasha's bedroom followed me like a shadow all morning. Every time I turned around, there it was, along with the mystery of the filled-in math answers.

By lunch I was driving myself crazy thinking about it. I needed to focus on something else. When Emily sat down, I noticed she had Band-Aids on the palms of both hands.

"What happened to you?" I asked.

"I was practicing with Dad and forgot my goalie gloves," she said. When soccer season had begun this year, nobody on our team wanted to be goalie. Mr. Davis told Emily to be goalie for the sake of the team, even though she'd never played the position before.

"It looks worse than it is," Emily said. "They're just scrapes."

"You're really getting into this," I said.

Emily shrugged. "I don't know if I am, but Dad sure is."

Her words hung in the air. Suddenly I felt sad. Emily was learning things from her dad that I would never get to learn from mine.

Emily craned her neck and looked past me. I turned to see Scott and Turner across the cafeteria.

"Did you ask your Mom?" she asked.

"Oops."

Emily gave me a "get with it" look.

"Tonight," I promised.

I wasn't thinking about boys or pizza after school while I sat on the front steps of our house waiting for Sasha to come home. It was a chilly day, but the sun was out and it felt good. Sasha came down the sidewalk carrying her backpack. She gave me a funny look. She knew I was waiting for an explanation for what had happened that morning.

"How did you do it?" I asked as she came up the driveway.

"I don't know," she said, stopping at the bottom of the steps.

"Don't give me that," I said. "I heard you talking in your room. You asked for help making your bed."

Sasha looked down at the steps.

"Come on, tell me," I said.

"You won't believe me."

"If you tell the truth, I swear I will."

"The ghost," my sister said.

I stared at her. "Sasha . . ."

"*Told* you."

"There's no such thing."

"That's what *you* think." Sasha started up the steps.

Who filled in the quiz answers?

A shiver ran through me and I felt goose bumps rise on my arms. I put out my hand to stop her. "Wait. How do you know if you haven't seen it?"

"I already told you. I just do."

The math quiz . . .

Sasha's bed . . .

"How long have you known about it?" I asked, still not believing that I was having a serious conversation with my sister about a ghost who made beds.

"Since Mom started the star chart."

I blinked. "Ever since your bedroom's been neat?"

She nodded.

"The *ghost* has been doing it for you?"

"Uh-huh."

I wanted to laugh, but. . . . "What else does it do?"

"He's not an it," Sasha said. "He's a he. And I don't know what else he does."

"*He* just makes your bed and straightens your room?"

"That's all I ever wish for," my sister said.

"You have to *wish*?"

"Yes."

This was absurd. "You're sure it's not a big blue genie and you have to rub a —"

Another thought left me unable to finish the sentence. Just before the girl from the Tigers made that "miracle miss," I'd wished for something.

And I'd wished for it again during the math quiz. And last night before Mom's date.

Suddenly my chest felt tight and it was hard to breathe. My heart was banging.

It couldn't really be. Could it?

12

Dinner that night took forever. I couldn't stop thinking about Dad.

If that's who the ghost really was.

If there really *was* a ghost.

But how else could you explain all the things that had happened?

Suppose it was true. That meant that Dad was still with us!

As a ghost? I thought I must be crazy.

But just suppose . . . It meant we hadn't lost him after all! I was excited and happy and scared and filled with so many emotions that it was almost impossible to eat.

"Something wrong, Kel?"

"Huh?"

"You've done nothing but stare out at the tree house since we sat down," Mom said. "You've hardly touched your food."

I glanced down at the orange mound of macaroni

and cheese on my plate. Normally I would have devoured it. But today was anything but normal.

"What if ghosts really do exist?" I asked.

Mom looked back at me without answering for a moment. Then she said, "What do you mean, hon?"

"I mean, what if they really *do* exist?"

"You know they don't."

"How can you be so sure?" I asked.

"It's just something I know," Mom said softly. "No matter how much we wish, when people die they don't come back."

I looked at Sasha, who looked at Mom.

"They do too!" my sister said. "And it's not just *any* ghost. *It's Dad!*"

Silence filled the kitchen.

Plink . . . plink.

Mom stared at Sasha with a perplexed look.

"At least, we *think* it's Dad," I said.

"You *said* it was him," Sasha stated.

"I said I *thought* it was him," I corrected her.

"What are you two talking about?" Mom asked.

I felt my face grow hot with nervousness. "You're not going to believe this, Mom, but something's going on. We think it might be Dad. He's been doing things."

Mom's eyes started to mist over.

"No, Mom! Don't get upset," I gasped. "Please. It's good. Honest. It means Dad's still with us!"

Mom dabbed her eyes with the cuff of her blouse. "You poor kids."

"No! No! Mom!" Sasha and I chanted together.

"We're not making this up," I said. "He really does things for us."

I told her how the answers to my math quiz had been filled in.

"Quiz answers?" Sasha stared at me.

Oops! I'd planned to keep that a secret.

"I thought he just cleaned up and made beds," my sister said.

"What?" Mom laughed nervously.

"He makes her bed and straightens her room every morning," I explained. "That's how she got all those stars."

Mom smiled archly. "A ghostly cleaning service?"

"We're serious," I said.

Mom turned to Sasha. "Have you finished dinner?"

She nodded.

"Run upstairs and start your homework," Mom said. "Kelly and I will do the dishes."

"Kelly has to do them alone," my sister said. "She lost a bet."

That darn kid never forgot anything.

Mom waited until she heard Sasha's footsteps go up the stairs. Then she turned to me and shook her head sadly. "Please, hon. Don't do this. Don't encourage her."

"Mom, I didn't —"

"You told her this ghost was your father?"

"Yes, but —"

"She's only eight years old. Don't you see how hurtful this could be? Encouraging her to think her father is a ghost?"

"Then who's been making her bed and straightening her room all this time?" I asked.

The lines in Mom's forehead deepened. "She must be."

"No way," I said. "Every morning she wishes for it. I've heard her. Then she walks out of the bedroom and it's done."

Mom stared at me and didn't say anything.

"I'm not lying," I said.

She turned away. But in the kitchen window I could see the reflection of her face fall into sadness. She pressed her fingers against her temples. Before Dad died I couldn't remember her ever having a headache. Now she got them all the time.

"I didn't mean to make you sad, Mom," I said.

"I'm going upstairs, Kelly." She stood up slowly. "Do the dishes and make sure your homework is done."

She left.

13

After Dad died, it sometimes felt like things were out of control. It wasn't just the dirty dishes in the sink or the dust growing thick under the beds. It was stuff like missing the deadline for summer camp sign up and forgetting to buy a white blouse so I'd have the right thing to wear at the spring choir performance.

Sometimes I heard Mom on the phone with her friend Jeannette, talking about how hard it was to keep everything going. All the permission slips and applications and bills and school conferences and meetings and laundry and food shopping and doctor and dentist appointments and on and on and on.

But suppose Dad really was back. What did it mean?

I was sitting on my bed, trying to concentrate on my homework, when someone knocked lightly on my door. I assumed it was Mom, since she hadn't really finished talking to me before.

"Come in," I said.

The door opened and Sasha came in. She stopped at the foot of my bed and whispered. "What did she say?"

"She thinks I'm encouraging you to believe that Dad is a ghost," I answered in a low voice. "Why'd you have to open your big mouth and tell her?"

"Because it's true."

There were moments when I believed it and moments when I thought we must be out of our minds. "Are you *positive* he makes your bed?"

"I'll show you," Sasha said. "I'll leave everything a total wreck. You get home from school before I do, so you'll see for yourself."

I shook my head. "No."

"Why not?"

"Because I don't think we should ask him to help us anymore."

Sasha studied me for a second. "Did he really take a test for you?"

"Don't get ideas," I warned her. "I didn't know about any ghosts. If I'd known he was going to do that, I never would have wished."

"Why not?" Sasha asked.

"Because it's not right," I said. "We may be fooling around with something, and we don't even know what it is. You *think* it's Dad, but what if it's not? What if it's something that's really bad?"

Sasha frowned. "But you said it was Dad."

"How would I know?" I asked. "I mean, what if it isn't? What if it's . . . some kind of . . . evil spirit that's just *pretending* to be Dad? What if it's keeping a record of all the things we're asking it to do, and then someday it's going to come back and say we owe it something in return?"

The lines between Sasha's eyebrows deepened. "Why?"

"I don't know *why*," I said. "I just know most kids don't have a ghost who makes beds and helps with quiz answers."

Sasha was quiet for a moment. Then she said, "You're right, Kel. They have *fathers*."

Rap! Rap! It was the door again.

"Come in, Mom," I said.

She came in. I held my breath while she focused on Sasha. "Aren't you supposed to be doing your homework?"

"Uh, I just wanted to talk to Kelly about something," Sasha replied.

"I hope it's not what I think," Mom said.

We both shook our heads. But Mom knew better.

Sasha and I played together sometimes, but it wasn't often that we just talked.

Mom told her to go back into her room. She waited until Sasha left and then leveled her gaze at me.

"I'm depending on you to do the right thing, Kel," she said.

I nodded and turned back to my homework.

A little while later I heard the water start to run in Mom's bathroom. Sometimes at night she took a hot bath to relax.

I waited until the water stopped running. Mom would be getting into the bathtub now. I got up and quietly went into Sasha's room. My sister was sitting at her desk, writing in a notebook. She looked up, surprised.

"What are you doing in here?" she whispered.

"Don't worry," I whispered back. "Mom's taking a bath. You have to promise not to use Dad anymore."

The corners of Sasha's mouth turned down. "Not ever?"

"Not ever," I said.

"What about in an emergency?" she asked.

"What kind of emergency?"

"Like I get lost or kidnapped or something and if

I don't get help something really bad will happen," she said.

I sighed. It was obvious that she wasn't going to give up.

"Okay, but *only* in an emergency," I said. "He'll be our emergency ghost."

14

The next morning at school Emily was waiting at my locker. Her hair was shiny and carefully brushed. "Did you ask?"

"About what?" I said.

Her jaw dropped. "Going for pizza with Scott and Turner. Don't tell me you forgot!"

"Sorry."

"How could you, Kel?" she asked. "My mom said I couldn't go unless your mom said you could go and now you don't know."

"I promise I'll ask tonight," I said.

"But the boys think we're going *today*," Emily said.

"We'll have to do it another time."

Emily looked seriously upset. "I can't believe you."

"Excuse me for saying this," I said, "but I thought you said Turner was too short."

"I changed my mind, okay?" she replied in a huff.

"He's cute and nice. His mom is famous . . . and he'll grow."

That night I asked Mom if I could go with Emily and the boys for pizza after school the next day. She said yes, provided I came straight home afterward. She even arranged for Sasha to go to a friend's house after school.

The following afternoon Emily, Scott, Turner, and I went into town. I walked with Scott, and Emily walked with Turner. Scott and I didn't say much on the way to Villa Maria. We mostly listened to Emily, who kept asking Turner about all the famous people his mother had met.

In Villa Maria, Emily and I sat side by side in a booth while the boys went to the counter to order.

"Isn't this cool?" Emily whispered.

"I guess," I whispered back uncertainly.

"What's bothering you?" She asked.

"I just wonder if you'd still like Turner if his mom wasn't on TV."

Emily pooh-poohed the thought. "Oh, come on. Of course."

The boys came back with a pitcher of soda and plastic cups.

"The pizza'll be ready in a few minutes," Scott said as he poured soda for each of us.

Emily leaned across the table toward Turner. "So who else has your mom met?"

Turner smiled politely. "Well, she once interviewed Arnold Schwarzenegger."

"Oh, wow! What was he like?"

"She said he was nice and funny."

"Who else?" Emily asked.

Turner's forehead wrinkled. I could see he wasn't keen on continuing the conversation.

"What was Kansas City like?" I asked.

Turner brightened and swept his dark hair out of his eyes. "Pretty cool. The only thing I didn't like was not being able to board. I'm really into it."

"So am I!" Emily exclaimed.

"Kansas isn't exactly known for its mountains," Turner said. "And with my mom's schedule, we only got to go at Christmas."

"Go where?" asked Scott.

"Aspen."

"Never heard of it," Scott said.

"I have!" Emily gasped. "It's in Colorado. All the movie stars have houses there!"

Was it my imagination, or was Emily suffering from a bad case of stars on the brain?

"You going this Christmas?" Scott asked.

Turner nodded.

"When you get back, you'll have to tell us about all the famous people you saw," Emily said.

Turner shifted uncomfortably in his seat. "Well, I may not come back, actually. At least not to this school."

Emily frowned. "What do you mean?"

"I'm applying to Country Day Academy," Turner said. "There's a chance they'll have room for me after Christmas. Otherwise I'm supposed to go next year."

Country Day was the local private school. The kids who went there came from families with lots of money. Emily, Scott, and I exchanged looks, but we didn't say anything. The weird thing was, I was surprised at how disappointed I felt.

It was starting to get dark by the time we finished our pizza. Outside the restaurant the boys said goodbye, and Emily and I walked home together. All she could talk about was Turner and movie stars and Aspen. I tried to listen, but as we neared my house, my thoughts turned to the ghost. Even though I'd decided that Sasha and I shouldn't use him, it was eerie to think he might somehow be there.

"So what do you think?" Emily asked, as we stopped on the sidewalk outside my house.

"Huh?" I didn't know what she was talking about.

"About boarding," she said.

"What about it?" I asked.

Emily put her hands on her hips. "Where have

you been, Kel? I was just talking about asking my dad to take us all boarding when there's snow."

"Oh, uh . . . okay."

Emily gave me a concerned look. "Are you all right?"

"Sure."

"See you at the game tomorrow?"

"Definitely."

Emily continued down the street. I went up the walk toward our house. Beyond it the sky had turned that last deep shade of blue before dark, and the first big bright star, which I knew was really Venus, was glimmering. I wondered again if Dad could really be with us. It made my heart ache. How I wished I could see him and touch him again.

15

The day was cold, gray, and windy. The sun would peek out from behind thick clouds for a second and then vanish for minutes at a time. Most of us were wearing turtlenecks under our soccer jerseys. Some of the girls even wore leggings under their soccer socks and shin guards.

I was sitting on the hard, cold ground. Emily was on her knees, tying my cleats the way Dad used to.

"I can't believe I'm doing this," she grumbled.

"Doesn't your dad do it for you?" I asked.

"Believe it or not, I know how to tie my own shoes," she said.

"All right, girls." Coach Bosky got our attention. "It's all or nothing today. Give it your best shot and" — for a moment he focused on me — "make sure you keep your minds on the game at all times."

Our opponents were the Cheetahs, the best team in the league. They were big and strong and kicked the ball really hard. It wouldn't be easy to beat them.

*   *   *

Halfway through the fourth quarter, with the score 2 to 1 in favor of the Cheetahs, I found myself standing in front of their goal, waiting to take a penalty kick.

Being a defender, I was rarely in scoring position, but Carrie Conners, our left wing, had sprained her knee, and Coach Bosky had chosen me to replace her. A few moments later I'd been tripped, and the ref had called an intentional foul.

"Give it a good one, Kel!" "You can do it!" "Tie the game for us, Kelly!" The shouts of support from my teammates and our friends on the sidelines rang in my ears.

The only thing between the ball and the goal was the Cheetahs' goalie, crouching, hands out, ready to dive.

The wind blew hard from behind, blowing my hair into my eyes. We needed this goal to stay alive, and it was up to me. My heart was pounding and my mouth was dry. The whole season rested on my shoulders. All the hopes of my teammates depended on this one kick. If I blew it, it would all be my fault.

I glanced at the sideline and imagined Dad there in his cowboy boots, jeans, and denim coat with the silver buttons. His hands would be jammed tightly into his pockets. I'd catch his eye and he'd nod as if to say, "You can do it, Kel."

I looked up. In the sky above us was a small dark

cloud with a halo of golden sunlight around it.

Please, Dad, I thought. *Help me make this score*.

Then I ran up and kicked the ball as hard as I could.

The ball soared into the air, but it was going straight toward the Cheetahs' goalie.

All she had to do was catch it.

She straightened up and raised her hands.

Suddenly the ball seemed to hop in the air. It sailed over her hands and into the net!

Tweet! The ref's whistle blew.

"Ya-hoo!" "Fantastic!" A roar rose from the sidelines. We'd scored! We'd tied the game!

The team crowded around, hugging me and patting my shoulders. "Way to go, Kel!" "Great shot!" Out of the corner of my eye, I saw the Cheetah's goalie with her head bowed. With her hands, she was demonstrating to her teammates how the ball had suddenly hopped in the air.

Then Coach Bosky was yelling at us: "Get into your positions, Leopards! The game's not over! We've tied. Now we have to win!"

With only seconds to go, Wendy Bosky, the coach's daughter, booted the ball high in the air and into the Cheetah net. The final score was 3 to 2. We won!

*　　*　　*

Mr. Davis drove Emily and me home after the game. As usual Mom had taken Sasha to ballet.

"You two were great!" In the car Mr. Davis was really pumped and excited. "Emily, you made some fantastic saves. And Kelly, that was . . . a super penalty kick. I don't know how you did it, but you saved the game."

"Don't say that, Dad," Emily playfully scolded him. "She made a totally great kick."

"Yeah, but the way it rose in the air," Mr. Davis said wondrously. "I don't know . . . must've been the wind, I guess."

"Thanks." I forced a smile on my face.

Was it the wind?

16

That night Emily came over for dinner. Mom ordered in a pizza.

"You beat the *Cheetahs*?" Sasha gasped, wide-eyed, when we told them about the game. "I thought they were the best team in the league!"

"Not anymore." I winked at Emily.

Mom had been nibbling on a piece of Sasha's crust. "I wish I could have been there. Was it close?"

"It couldn't have been any closer," Emily said. Then she told how I'd saved the game with the penalty kick. "My dad said he'd never seen the ball do that."

"Do what?" Mom asked.

Emily explained how the ball had been heading straight for the Cheetahs' goalie when it unexpectedly hopped over her hands.

"The *really* weird thing is, it's the second time in the playoffs that something like that has happened," Emily said.

Uh-oh! Suddenly I felt Sasha's eyes on me.

"The *second* time?" Mom's eyebrows rose curiously.

Emily told her how, the week before, the girl on the Tigers missed that incredibly easy shot on the wide-open goal.

"I was the closest person to her," she said. "The ball was lined up perfectly. She had the whole goal to kick into. And at the very last second, the ball moved. It wasn't like she missed. It was like an invisible hand reached out and moved the ball."

I felt Sasha's glare burrowing into me.

"Maybe it hit a rock in the field," Mom said.

"That's what I thought, too," Emily said. "But after the game I went back to the spot. There was no rock. There was nothing except grass."

Mom was quiet for a moment. Then she said, "Well, it doesn't matter now. The great thing is that the Leopards won and get to play in the championship. Sasha, I know you have ballet on Saturdays, but I really don't want to miss Kelly's last game. How about we watch her and then go? You'll be late for ballet. But I think that's okay for one week, don't you?"

My sister had been glaring at me nonstop. "Sure, Mom. I wouldn't want to miss that game for *anything*."

*   *   *

"Some emergency," Sasha grumbled later. We were in the kitchen doing the dishes. Emily had gone home.

"What are you talking about?" I asked innocently.

"First you made me promise not to use him except for emergencies," my sister said. "And then you went right ahead and used him in a *soccer* game."

"Did not."

"What about those two amazing things Emily told us about?"

"They just happened."

"You *sure* you didn't wish to Dad for them?"

"Uh . . ."

"What are you two arguing about now?" Mom asked as she came into the kitchen.

"Nothing, Mom," I said.

"If that was nothing," said Mom, "I'd hate to see how you fight over *something*."

Neither Sasha nor I replied.

"Okay, I have something to tell you," Mom said. "Remember that dinner I was supposed to have with Jason Stark?"

"The one where the car broke?" Sasha asked.

"Yes," Mom said and looked at me. "And before you say anything, Kel, I promise I'll have the oil changed and the tires checked."

"So what about Mr. Stark?" I asked.

"We're going to try again this Tuesday," Mom

said. "There's no school on Wednesday because of teachers conferences. Kristen will baby-sit you again."

Sasha and I locked eyes. I had the feeling we were both thinking the same thing. *What about Dad?*

I mean, *if* he really was around . . .

"Maybe it's not such a good idea, Mom," Sasha said.

"Why not?" Mom asked.

"Well, you know. . . . Dad."

Mom took a deep breath and let it out slowly. "Hon, I will always love your father. No matter what happens. Mr. Stark and I are just going out for dinner."

"But why?" Sasha asked.

"To spend some grown-up time together," Mom said. "To talk. To compare notes about being single parents."

"Why don't you compare notes on the phone?" my sister asked. "That way you won't have to get dressed up, and you'll save a lot of money on dinner."

Mom smiled for a second. But it disappeared quickly. "I'm sorry, kids. I know this upsets you. But it's something I have to do. For me."

17

On Tuesday night, Sasha and I were in the den watching TV when Mom came in. She was wearing a red dress and makeup, and she smelled of perfume. For once her hair was combed out rather than pulled back in a ponytail.

"You smell nice, Mom," I said.

"Thanks. Kristen just arrived, so I'm going to go. Where's Emily?"

Since there was no school the next day, Emily and I had decided to have a sleepover.

"She's coming after dinner," I said. "Where are you and Mr. Stark going?"

"We're going to try La Reserve again."

"Like last time?" Sasha asked.

"It better *not* be like last time," Mom said. "Last time we never even got to see each other."

She kissed us both and told us to behave ourselves. She promised she'd be back by ten o'clock and said we could stay up if we wanted.

As soon as Mom left, Sasha said, "Want to bet Dad had something to do with Mom not making it to the restaurant last time?"

Knowing I'd wished for precisely that, I shook my head. I didn't want her to know. "Doesn't matter. We're not using him anymore, remember?"

"Yeah, right. Except for *your* soccer games." Sasha gazed up at the ceiling. "Dad? Listen, I know Mom thinks she needs companionship and everything, but that's because she doesn't know you're still around. Could you make sure she doesn't have a good time tonight? Thanks."

Was it my imagination, or did the den brighten for a moment?

No, it was probably just the light from the TV.

Emily came over and we watched a video, then played with my dollhouse. I let Sasha hang out with us. It always made her feel good to be included with us big kids.

"I was in the school yard at lunch today and guess who drove by with his mother?" Emily asked.

"Uh . . ." I pressed my finger against my lip and pretended that it was a tough question. "Turner?"

Emily nodded. "You should see their car."

"Who's Turner?" Sasha asked.

"A new boy in school," I said.

"Not just any new boy," Emily said. "His mother's Karen Gebhart, the new health and science editor on Channel Eight."

"Turner comes up to Emily's armpit," I added.

"So? Height's not the only thing," Emily said.

"Especially when your mom's rich and famous," I said.

Emily wrinkled her nose at me. "Anyway, it's long and green and has wire wheels."

"What is?" I asked.

"His *car*, silly."

"Wire wheels? Wouldn't they be better off with rubber?"

"Not the *tires*," Emily said impatiently. "The *wheels*. They're the things the tires go on."

"Well, *excuuuuse* me," I said. "I didn't know you were such a car expert."

"Actually, Scott told me about the wheels," Emily admitted.

"So what about them?" Sasha asked.

"Only really expensive foreign cars have them," Emily explained.

"In other words, Turner's mom has a really expensive foreign car," I said.

"Can you imagine?" Emily asked dreamily.

"Imagine what?" Sasha asked.

"Your mom's on TV all the time. You go skiing in Aspen and drive around in a fancy car."

"With wire wheels," I added.

"Sounds cool," said Sasha.

"So, did you run out into the street and throw yourself in front of the car to make sure Turner saw you?" I asked.

Emily made a face. "Very funny, Kel. They just drove by. She was probably taking him out to lunch. I bet his mom hardly ever cooks."

I winked at Sasha. "If that's what it takes to be famous, our mom must be a superstar."

"So your mom's going out with that guy again?" Emily asked. "Is it serious?"

"Not yet," I said. "They didn't actually meet last time."

"So you don't know what he looks like?" Emily asked.

Sasha and I shook our heads.

"Must be weird," Emily said.

"Kel and I aren't worried," Sasha suddenly said. "It's not going to work out."

I gave her a look.

"How do you know?" Emily asked.

"We just know." Sasha smiled.

Emily gave me a curious glance. I shrugged. "She doesn't know what she's talking about."

"Do too!" Sasha insisted.

I gritted my teeth and glowered at her. Emily gave both of us a puzzled look but didn't say anything more.

18

Dad had been an early riser and made breakfast for us every morning. He would do the dishes every night, vacuum the house once a week, and help with the laundry. With those things taken care of, Mom was able to do the rest even though she worked full time.

Except for his business trips, he was always there.

If we were having a hard time with our homework, he'd help. If we needed a ride to a friend's house or to the movies, he'd drive. If we were upset and needed someone to talk to, he'd always stop what he was doing and listen.

If we made a mess, he'd help us clean up. If we left something somewhere, we could count on him to go get it. He didn't come only to my soccer games. He came to a lot of the practices, too.

Sometimes I wanted to be alone with a friend or just do something by myself. Dad would start making the usual suggestions: Did I want to go to a movie? Have a catch? Work on the dollhouse we were building together? Play Sorry? Checkers? Gin rummy?

I'd just smile up at him and say, "Hey, Dad, get a life."

It was our private little joke, my way of letting him know I loved him but couldn't spend every free moment with him.

It wasn't until after he died that I realized how our family was like a wheel. In some ways Dad was the hub and Mom, Sasha, and I were the spokes. As long as we were attached to him, we worked fine. But without him, we sometimes fell apart.

At 10:05 we heard the front door open. Emily, Sasha, and I were still up in my room. Sasha dashed to the top of the stairs and called down. "How'd it go?"

"Don't ask," Mom groaned from the front hall. "It's time for you to go to bed. I'll be up as soon as I pay Kristen."

Sasha turned back to Emily and me with a triumphant smile on her face. "See, I told you something would go wrong." Then she went into her room.

I felt a wave of nervousness wash through me.

It must have been Dad.

"That's weird," said Emily. "How'd she know?"

"You got me." I pretended not to have a clue.

Emily squinted at me. "You look pale, Kel."

"Oh, uh . . . I must be tired," I said.

We heard Mom downstairs asking Kristen if everything went okay. Kristen said it did, but how she knew was a mystery since she hadn't left the couch or looked up from her homework all night. Mom paid her and then came upstairs. Before going into Sasha's room, she poked her head into mine. "You and Emily ought to get into bed, too."

We nodded. She went to read to Sasha.

"Tell me what happened," we heard Sasha say.

"I won't bore you," Mom said.

"Oh, come on. Please?"

"I don't know why you'd care."

"Come on, Mom," Sasha begged. "I just want to know."

"Oh, okay."

In a flash Emily and I were on our feet. We huddled near my doorway and listened as Mom told Sasha that she and Mr. Stark had managed to meet at La Reserve, but then disaster struck. The waiter dropped a bowl of soup in Mr. Stark's lap. Mr. Stark said he'd go home to change, but out in the parking lot he discovered that all *four* of his tires were flat. So Mom had to drive him home, and then back to the restaurant to have his car towed to a garage. By then it was time for Mom to leave.

"If I didn't know better, I'd swear someone was

trying to make sure Mr. Stark and I never have dinner together," Mom said.

"That wouldn't surprise me," Sasha replied.

Emily gave me a funny look, but I pretended not to notice.

"What do you mean?" Mom asked.

"Oh, nothing," Sasha said.

"Well, it's getting late," Mom said. "What should I read?"

"A ghost story, please?"

19

Thursday morning I was in my room after breakfast when I heard Sasha come up the stairs. She'd been a slowpoke again and I knew there was no way she could make her bed and straighten her room in time. I finished making my bed and stepped out into the hall. Sasha's door was closed, but I could hear her inside. *"I wish you'd help me."*

I quickly knocked on her door and pushed it open. Sasha spun around and stared at me with wide, surprised eyes. Her bed wasn't made and her pajamas were in a pile on the floor.

"Remember what we agreed?" I said. "Only if it's an emergency."

"Or soccer," she reminded me.

"Okay, I shouldn't have done it," I admitted. "But you shouldn't have messed around with Mom's date, either. So we're even and that's the end of it."

Sasha pursed her lips angrily. "Just because *you* don't want his help doesn't mean I can't ask."

"Oh, darn!" Mom muttered from downstairs. "There goes the bus. Come on, girls, I'll have to drive you."

I left my sister's room, hurried down the stairs, and ran out to the Dirtmobile.

A moment later, Sasha got in.

"You have everything?" Mom asked as she steered out of the driveway.

"Yes," Sasha replied.

"Bed made and room straightened?" Mom asked.

I twisted around and stared at Sasha over the seat, waiting for her reply.

Sasha crossed her arms stubbornly and tucked her chin against her chest. She glared back at me. "You bet, Mom."

"I told you not to use him anymore," I said after school. I was standing in Sasha's room. It was spotless; the bed was made perfectly, clothes put away.

"Who made you the boss?" Sasha asked. She was sitting on the floor, playing with a small, white bear. Now that it was the fall, we didn't get many sunny days, but today the late afternoon sun was streaming in her window.

"We had a deal," I said.

"No, we didn't."

"Yes, we did," I said. "You were just too lazy to

get up in time to make your bed and clean your room."

My sister bent her head and sniffed. A tear gathered in her eyelash, then rolled down her cheek, leaving a wet trail.

"Oh, come on, it's nothing to cry about," I said.

"I want him." She wiped the tears off her cheeks with her hand.

"Huh?"

"I want him to come back," she sobbed. "Right now."

"He can't," I said.

Sasha glared at me through her tears. "You just don't want him to!"

"What are you talking about?"

"You don't want me to use him," Sasha wailed. "You want to keep him all to yourself!"

"No, Sasha, what's with you?"

My sister squeezed her eyes shut. "I wish you were here, Daddy. Please come here. I miss you so much. Daddy, give me a hug."

"No!" I gasped.

"Yes! *Please?*" Sasha begged, with her eyes still closed.

The room became quiet. Even with the sun coming in the window, it seemed brighter than normal.

Sasha stopped crying. Her shoulders loosened and

her head started to tilt. She began to relax and lean to one side. Farther . . . farther . . . She was leaning far enough that she should have fallen over.

But she just stayed there.

Leaning.

As if someone was holding her.

I realized I'd stopped breathing. My heart was pounding inside my chest. I whispered hoarsely. "Sasha?"

She didn't answer. Her hands were crossed loosely in her lap. Her legs were tucked to the side as if she was nestling in someone's lap. Her eyes were still closed, but her expression was serene and comforted.

The room felt warm and light.

"Dad?" The word left my throat in a quavering whisper.

Sasha opened her eyes. "Let him stay, Kel. Please?"

Seconds passed slowly. Sasha stayed in that impossible angle with her eyes closed. The room was so quiet. The only sound was my breath.

I should have been scared.

But I wasn't. Not really. Nervous and excited was more like it. Was it really possible that Dad was here?

Sasha's body began to tilt back up. She opened her eyes, as if caught by surprise. After a moment, she was sitting upright again.

"What happened?" I whispered.

"He finished hugging me," she said.

"What . . . did it feel like?"

Sasha shook her head. "I don't know. It wasn't like a regular hug, but something was here."

"Is he still here?" I asked.

"I don't know," she said. "Did you want him to hug you?"

"*No!*" The word came out with such force that it surprised me. I felt bad. "Oh, Dad, it's not that I *don't* want you to hug me," I said, looking up at the wall. "It's just that I'm scared."

"It didn't hurt," Sasha said.

"I know," I answered. "It's hard to explain. It's scary . . . even if it is you, Dad. Don't be mad, please?"

"I don't think he's mad," Sasha said. "I bet he's just happy to be with us."

I looked around, wishing I could catch a glimpse of him. But all I saw was sunlight slanting through the windows, catching the little specks of dust floating in the air.

"I can't believe I'm believing this," I whispered.

"Isn't it great?" Sasha asked.

"Yes . . . I guess . . . I don't know."

Sasha scowled.

"I mean, it's so weird." On impulse, I reached for the small white bear Sasha had been playing with. I held it in my open palm. "Dad, if you're still here, take this from me."

I held my breath. For a moment nothing happened. Then the bear leaned forward and fell out of my hand.

"Oh, my gosh!" I gasped as it tumbled to the floor.

Sasha beamed. The fact that there might a ghost in her room didn't seem to bother her at all. I looked around the sunlit room again, yearning to see some sign of him among the books and stuffed bears, but everything was still and quiet.

Except my heart, which was pounding like crazy.

"Dad," I said, "I just want you to know that I love you as much as ever. I really miss you and I'm totally glad you're back, even if I can't see you. And I really hope you're not mad that I didn't want you to hug me. I'm just a little freaked by this. Please try to understand. You and Mom taught us what to do in a lot of weird situations, but you have to admit that meeting a ghost wasn't one of them."

Silence and sunlight. The flecks of dust hung effortlessly in the air.

"Do you think he's trying to answer?" I asked Sasha.

"I don't know," she said.

I had an idea and held out my hand. "Dad, if you

still love us and miss us, maybe you'd hold my hand?"

I felt a strange sensation and instantly jerked my hand away. But then I slowly reached out again. Something went around my hand. It felt like warm pressure, as if my hand was in sunlight and the air around it had gotten thick.

A thrill raced through me.

"You understand why it scares me to get hugged?" I asked.

The feeling of warmth stayed. Sunlight brightened the room, but it wasn't shining directly on my hand.

It just felt like it was.

"But you know that I love you more than anything in the world, right?" I asked.

It was still there.

"Do you feel it?" Sasha asked.

I nodded. Like Mom, I always tried to be strong and never let anyone see me cry, but now the tears just rolled down my cheeks.

I couldn't let go.

20

The soccer championship was rained out that weekend, but I hardly cared. Sasha and I stayed in the house, warmed by the glow of Dad's presence.

On Monday morning Sasha stayed in bed late again.

"Sasha!" Mom called from the kitchen while I finished a bowl of Cheerios. "Get down here right now or you'll miss the bus! And this time I am *not* driving you to school under *any* circumstances!"

It sounded like she was in a bad mood. She put down her coffee mug and pressed her fingers against her temples.

"Headache?" I asked.

She nodded. "All weekend."

"Anything I can do?" I asked.

"Yes, go straighten your room," she said. "And while you're upstairs, see what's keeping your sister *this* time."

I'd just climbed the stairs when Sasha came out of her room. Her bed was unmade and her pajamas were on the floor.

I went into my room. Like Sasha's it was a mess. The bed was a wreck, and clothes from the weekend were scattered all over the place. My books were everywhere. I really didn't feel like cleaning it all up. I gathered my books, stuffed them into my backpack, and went downstairs.

Mom looked surprised. "Room straightened already?"

"Uh, yup."

"That was fast," she said.

"Guess I'm getting good at it," I replied.

Mom looked up at the kitchen clock. "The bus is going to be here any second. Come on, kids, time to go."

Sasha and I grabbed our coats and went out the door with Mom. It was wet, cold, and gray outside. Soggy brown and yellow leaves blanketed the ground, and white plumes of vapor escaped our lips with every breath.

"Brrrr. Have a good day at school, girls." Mom stopped at the bottom of the front steps and kissed us both on the forehead. Then she got into the Dirtmobile and left for work.

Sasha and I started to walk down the sidewalk toward the bus stop.

"So?" I said.

"So . . . what?"

"Did you?"

"Did I what?"

"You know," I said.

Sasha played dumb. "I don't know what you're talking about."

"Aren't you going to ask him to make your bed?"

She pretended to be surprised. "You're right! I forgot!" Then she stopped right there on the sidewalk and shut her eyes.

"Wait!" I said.

Sasha opened her eyes. "What?"

"Could you ask him for me, too?" I asked sheepishly.

We collected gold stars every morning that week without making our beds once. The garbage was taken out, the laundry hamper emptied, and the kitchen chores done without our lifting a finger. On Thursday night Mom dashed across the street to Jeannette's for her book group meeting. I sat in my room and did my homework until bedtime, while Sasha watched TV.

On Friday morning Sasha came downstairs carrying a large hand-drawn poster report on Colorado.

"Sasha, that's beautiful!" Mom gushed while my sister beamed. "When did you do it?"

"Last night," Sasha replied.

I gave her a look of disbelief.

She stuck out her tongue at me.

"I don't know about this," I said later at the bus stop. "I mean, I guess it's okay if he makes our beds. But you're supposed to do your own homework. That's how you learn. Are you just going to have Dad do *everything* for you?"

My sister shook her head. "Not everything. Just the things I don't have time to do myself."

"You could have done your homework if you hadn't watched TV all night," I said.

"But Dad always helped us with projects and reports," Sasha said.

"Sure, he *helped* us, but he didn't *do* them for us," I replied.

"I worked on it, too," Sasha said.

"How?" I asked.

"I picked which state to do," she explained.

I rolled my eyes. "You are totally unbelievable. I mean, how do you think Dad feels about being used like this?"

"I bet he feels good," my sister said. "It always made him feel good to help us before. Why should it be any different now?"

"Because now it seems like that's *all* you want him for."

I was shocked to see Sasha's eyes grow watery. "That's not true! When I ask him to do something and he does it, it makes me feel like he's still here."

She wiped the corners of her eyes with her fingers. "Then I don't miss him as much. So don't tell me not to ask him to do stuff, Kel, 'cause that's the only way I know he's still around."

She wiped her eyes, then turned away and went down the sidewalk so that she could be alone. Was she right? I knew the part about not missing him as much was true. I felt it, too. But how could we ask him to do everything for us?

That wasn't right, was it?

21

One night in fifth grade, before Dad died, I was on the phone for hours. Scott had called, making him the first boy ever to call me. And after we finished talking I immediately called Emily to tell her about Scott. Then a boy named Jeremy Spence called to find out what I thought of Scott, and that led to another call to Emily. Finally Mom said I had to get off the phone and finish my homework.

I was sitting on my bed doing social studies when Dad knocked on the door and came in. He was wearing his little reading glasses and had an odd sort of smile on his face.

"Heard a boy called," he said.

I felt my face turn red.

"Guess I always knew this day would come," he said, sitting down on the edge of my bed.

"What day?" I asked, although inside I knew.

Dad took off the glasses and put them in his shirt pocket. "You've discovered boys."

"Dad, I've known about boys for a long time," I said, still playing dumb, mostly because I was embarrassed.

"But until now they were just other kids to play with," Dad said. "Not much different from girls except that their hair was shorter and they didn't like dolls. Now it's different, isn't it?"

"Well . . . sort of." What was the use in pretending?

Dad nodded. Oddly, he looked kind of pleased, which didn't make sense to me at all. "Listen, I know this feels very important and exciting. But I don't want you to forget that the reason you're in school is to learn, not to have a social life."

Then he winked.

My face still felt warm. I knew he was right, and I felt good that he hadn't been angry or anything. He understood.

The sixth grade was going on a field trip to the science center. When I got to school, two empty buses were parked at the curb. Mr. Palmer, the assistant principal, stood on the sidewalk holding a clipboard in one hand and a megaphone in the other.

"If your last name begins with A through L, you're

on bus number one," he announced through the megaphone. "M through Zs are on bus two."

I was on bus number one. I didn't mind. Emily's last name was Davis, so I'd get to sit with her.

"Go ahead and get on, Kelly," Mr. Palmer said, checking off my name on his clipboard.

I waited while Carrie Conners hobbled on with her crutches. Her leg was in a soft cast, covered with signatures and doodles. Seeing her reminded me of the upcoming soccer league championship game. Coach Bosky had told me that I'd be playing left wing again.

I climbed on the bus and went down the aisle. Emily was sitting by herself about two-thirds of the way back. When I got to her seat, she put her hand down on the empty spot and shook her head.

"I'm saving it for you-know-who," she whispered. "Scott's on the other bus, so Turner will have no one to sit with."

I was shocked. "Are you serious?"

"I really want to sit with him, Kel," she said. "Don't be mad, okay?"

No, it wasn't okay. I was mad. Emily and I had been best friends for a long time. I wanted to sit with *her*. Besides, Emily didn't care about Turner. All she cared about was his famous mother and Aspen and wire wheels.

I sat down in a seat two rows in front of her. Boy, was I steaming. This was just too much. What was with her? Had she gone completely boy-crazy?

Through the bus window, I saw Turner arrive. All at once I had an idea. I closed my eyes. *Dad, can you make Turner sit with me? Please? I wish you would.*

Suddenly I felt the strangest sensation. I couldn't be certain what it was, but it *felt* like Dad didn't want to do it. Like he was trying to resist my wish.

Wait a minute! It wasn't that I really wanted to sit with Turner. I just wanted to show Emily.

"Oh, come on, Dad! It's a field trip, okay? It's not like I'm going to be doing any schoolwork on the bus."

I could actually feel Dad struggling. It reminded me of all those times when we'd ask him to do something for us, and he'd resist, saying that we really should learn to do it ourselves. Of course, he always wound up doing it anyway.

"This is no fair! I just want to sit with him."

I felt a finger tap me on the shoulder. "Uh, Kel?"

I jumped with surprise, then opened my eyes. Emily had reached over the seat between us and tapped me on the shoulder. Everyone around us was staring at me.

"Why are you talking to yourself?" she whispered.

"Uh, I didn't know I was," I stammered.

"You said something about sitting with someone,"

she said. "It sounded like you were having an argument."

"Oh, uh, it was just something I was remembering from this morning," I quickly replied.

Meanwhile Turner climbed on the bus, and Emily instantly forgot about me.

"Hi, Turner!" She waved.

Turner waved back and came down the aisle. Once again, I shut my eyes. Only this time I made sure I wished silently: *Please, Dad?*

I opened my eyes and glanced at Emily. She was beaming with the expectation that Turner was going to sit with her. But as he came toward the seat where I was sitting, he suddenly stopped and looked as if he hadn't noticed me before. "Oh, hi, Kelly."

"Hi." I smiled up at him. Was it my imagination, or did the bus grow brighter inside?

"Anyone sitting there?" he asked, pointing to the empty spot beside me.

I shook my head.

Turner sat down.

Next to me.

We talked all the way to the science center. It turned out that Turner didn't hear much from his father now that his parents were divorced. When Turner found out that my dad had died, it sort of gave us something in common. And even though his mom was famous and mine wasn't, they both worked, and that gave us even more to talk about, like which brands of frozen microwave pizza were the best. As the bus pulled into the parking lot and stopped, Turner turned to me.

"Thanks," he said.

"For what?" I asked uncertainly.

"For not asking me once about what famous people my mother knows."

As soon as we got off the bus, Turner hooked up with Scott, who'd just gotten off the other bus. Emily sidled up to me and shot a few eye daggers in my direction.

"I wanted him to sit with me," she muttered as we followed the crowd into the science center.

"It wasn't like I asked him to sit with me," I whispered back. "He just decided to."

"But I heard you before he sat down. You were saying something about wanting someone to sit with you. Who were you talking to?"

"No one, Em, really."

But Emily just gave me a look. I knew she didn't believe me.

22

"Homework all done?" Mom stood in the den doorway. She'd just come home from work.

Without taking our eyes off the TV, Sasha and I both nodded.

"You sure?" Mom asked.

"Yes, Mom," we answered in unison.

A little later she called us for dinner. Sasha and I went into the kitchen and sat down to eat.

Usually Mom was full of questions about our day, but that night she was quiet as we slurped up chunky chicken noodle soup.

Finally, she said, "Something's bothering me, girls."

Sasha and I both looked up.

"Your backpacks are lying right next to the front door where you always leave them when you get home."

Sasha and I exchanged guilty looks. *Busted!*

"I don't know what to say." Mom sounded disappointed. "I don't want to accuse you of lying about your homework, and I'm not going to ask to see it. But I think you'll have to agree that it's *extremely* unusual for you to have done your homework and put your backpacks by the front door."

Sasha squeezed her eyes closed. Her lips moved silently. I knew what she was doing — wishing Dad to do her homework for her.

"What was that about?" Mom asked her when she opened her eyes.

"Nothing," Sasha replied innocently.

Mom frowned.

"I'm sorry, Mom," I said. "I'll go up and do my homework right after dinner."

Mom just nodded but didn't say anything more. When dinner ended she said she was going upstairs to take a bath.

"I'd like you to do the dishes, kids," she said. "And let's try to keep the TV off tonight."

"Just *one* show?" Sasha begged.

"Okay, one show." Mom gave in, then turned to me. "But I really want all your homework done first, Kel, okay?"

"You bet."

Mom left.

"I want to go upstairs and start my homework," I said to Sasha. "Would you do the dishes?"

My sister looked around to make sure Mom had

gone. "Why don't we just get Dad to do them?" she asked in a low voice.

"I don't want to," I replied. "I really don't think it's right."

"Okay, go ahead," Sasha said.

I got my backpack and went up to my room. A few minutes later Sasha came upstairs and went into her room. There was no way she'd had time to do the dishes and straighten the kitchen. It wasn't hard to guess what had happened.

But it made me wonder. Why did I resist letting Dad do stuff for me now that he was a ghost? I'd never minded when he was alive.

For the next hour I did homework. The house was quiet. Usually the phone rang after dinner, and it would be Emily asking for help with homework, but really calling to talk. Tonight the phone didn't ring. She and I hadn't said a word to each other since the field trip to the science center.

Later I heard Sasha's door open again. It was just before 8:30, which meant she was going to watch TV. I'd done everything except my math, which was taking forever. I liked my other subjects, but math was a pain. Besides, I'd asked Dad to do it for me so many times lately that it was hard to figure out what was going on.

I'd promised Mom I wouldn't watch TV unless all my homework was done.

But I really wanted to watch.

Hey, Dad, I did most of my homework myself. It's just the math that's slowing me up. Do you think you could help?

I was surprised when I felt resistance.

Oh, come on, Dad.

But the resistance was still there. After days of doing my math homework, why was he hesitating now?

Look, this isn't fair. One of the reasons it's so hard is because you've been doing it. You can't just dump it all on me now.

I felt his resistance start to waver.

Come on, just for tonight. I promise I'll do it myself tomorrow. I swear!

The resistance disappeared. I packed up my books and went into the den to watch. Sasha was sitting crosslegged on the floor.

"Finish your homework?" she asked.

I nodded and felt guilty. It was wrong to have Dad do my homework. This was definitely the last time I was going to ask.

23

The next morning Emily was waiting by my desk when I got to Ratsky's class.

"Let's not fight, okay?" she said.

"I didn't start it, Em," I said.

"I know." Emily's shoulders sagged a little. "I was just mad because Turner sat with you and not me."

"It's not like I made him do it," I said. Little did she know . . .

"I'd still like to know who you were arguing with about letting a 'him' sit with you," Emily said.

"I told you, no one."

"I've never seen you talk to yourself before," she said.

It was definitely time to change the subject. "Have you talked to Turner since then?"

"No," Emily said. "Have *you*?"

"No."

"Maybe we could get Scott and him to go out for pizza again," she said.

"If you want." I tried to act like I didn't care. But I did. I wanted to see Turner again.

Ratsky came in and started class.

"Let's review, ladies and gentlemen," he announced, writing a problem on the board. "Who knows what to do when a percentage is not a whole number?"

The class sat there dumbly.

Ratsky's forehead wrinkled. "Oh, come on, we went over this two days ago." When no hands went up, he turned to me. "Okay, Kelly, tell them."

"Uh, sorry?" Why was he picking *me*?

Ratsky put his hands on his hips. "Tell them what you do when the percentage isn't a whole number."

I blinked nervously. Ratsky furrowed his eyebrows. "Remember the extra credit?"

I bit my lip and shook my head.

Ratsky turned to the rest of the class. "You always round to the nearest tenth," he said, as if it was obvious. Then he glanced back at me with a puzzled look.

I didn't even *know* I'd done the extra credit.

"Kelly, could I speak to you for a moment?" Ratsky said. The bell had just rung. Kids were leaving the classroom. I told Emily to go ahead and I'd catch up to her.

"There's something I don't understand," Ratsky

said, once we were alone. "Two nights ago the homework extra credit was to round percentages to the nearest tenth. You were the only one in class who did it without a mistake."

"Guess I forgot," I said.

Ratsky just stared at me. It must've sounded like a pretty feeble excuse. "All right, Kelly. You'd better get to your next class."

Gladly.

24

It was the day after Halloween and the Leopards were playing the Impalas in the league championship game. It was a sunny day and warmer than normal. The biggest crowd of the year stood on the sidelines. Carrie Conners was there on her crutches. Mom and Sasha were there.

"Where's your dad?" I asked Emily, as we stretched before the game.

"He had to go to a sales meeting," she said. "Can you believe it? The most important game of the year and he can't be here."

"Bummer," I said. "And after all the work he's done with you at goalie."

"Well, let's just win today," she said. "Then I'll be able to tell him all about it."

"Piece of cake," I said.

It should have been a piece of cake. We'd beaten the Impalas easily during the regular season. But now in the championship game we must have been overconfident, because it wasn't long before we were losing 2 to 0.

"This is your last chance," Coach Bosky warned us at halftime. "We didn't come all this way to lose. Now go out there and win!"

We managed to score two goals in the second half, tying the game. Meanwhile, the Impalas nearly scored again, but Emily made a fantastic dive to deflect the ball before it went into our goal.

I was standing near the Impalas' sideline when she did it, and I could hear everyone on their side groan with frustration and then utter words of grudging admiration. I wanted to tell them that Emily was my best friend. And just to rub it in, I wanted to add that she didn't even know how to be a goalie when the season started!

After Emily's save, you could almost feel the tone of the game change. It was still tied, but somehow we knew we were going to win.

With less than a minute to go, we had a corner kick. I positioned myself in front of the Impalas' goal. This was the perfect opportunity to score.

And a score here would make us the league champions!

Dad would be so proud. Emily's dad, too.

Dad? Help me score? I knew I shouldn't have asked, but everyone wanted to win so badly.

I was surprised when I felt him resist. Again.

Oh, come on, Dad. It's the last game of the year. The championship! Don't you want us to win?

The resistance was still there.

I can't believe you! You really want us to lose?

Suddenly I felt the warmth of the sun glowing down on the top of my head.

Wendy Bosky took the corner kick and booted the ball into the air toward the goal.

It was coming right toward me, but it was too high! I knew I was supposed to head it into the goal, but I'd never done that. I wasn't even certain I could jump high enough to reach it.

I jumped.

Suddenly I felt as if something lifted me a few extra inches!

The ball was sailing toward me and I jerked my head sideways.

Slap! The ball hit me on the left side of the head.

Thump! I hit the ground.

A roaring cheer went up. A burning sensation throbbed through my head and my left ear stung. Then I felt hands helping me up. People were shouting my name.

"Kelly, you did it!" "Incredible!" "We won!"

Everyone went crazy. My header had been the winning score! We were the league champions!

Filled with excitement and joy, we all raced to the

sideline, where our parents were cheering. Everyone crowded around us.

Coach Bosky actually hugged me! "Kelly, that was great!"

I was glowing with pride. Mom and Sasha pressed toward me through the crowd.

"I never knew you were so good!" Mom gushed. "That was fantastic!"

Sasha shook my hand. "Nice going, slug-face."

Mom hugged me. "I'm so proud of you. I wish I could stay, but I have to take Sasha to ballet and we're late. I'll see you at home later, okay?"

"Sure thing."

Mom hurried off with Sasha. We lined up to shake hands with the Impalas. Some of them even congratulated me on my header. Back on the sideline, Coach Bosky said he'd see us all at the league soccer dinner, where we'd get our championship trophies.

Both teams began to drift away from the field. Over in the parking lot, kids were getting into their parents' cars and going home or out to celebrate. But I found it hard to leave. Mom and Sasha wouldn't be home, and the house would be empty— the way it felt after Dad died.

The sun was still high in the sky. It was a beautiful fall day and it felt good to be the heroine. I stood in the sun, warmed by its glow.

"Kel?"

The sound of someone calling my name surprised me. I turned and found Emily behind me. A few tears rolled down her cheek.

"What's with you?" I asked.

Emily smiled through the tears. "I don't know. Either I'm really happy we won, or I'm really sad that my dad wasn't here to see it. But neither of those seem enough to make me cry, you know?"

I nodded.

Emily used the sleeve of her green-and-blue goalie jersey to wipe away her tears, leaving smudges on her cheeks. She grinned. "So maybe I'm just crying because . . . it's time to cry."

I put my arm around her shoulder, and together we started off the field.

"That was an amazing header," she said. "Another incredible play."

I started to nod proudly, then realized that I'd temporarily forgotten who was really responsible for that "incredible play." I didn't make the game-winning score alone. I'd had help.

"You're the person who really made the amazing play," I said. "That save set us up to win."

"Not that anyone remembers." Emily hung her head. "Coach Bosky didn't even mention it after the game."

"He was just excited about winning," I said. "Wait till you tell your dad. He'll be really proud of you."

"Your dad would be really proud of you, too," Emily replied.

Is he? I wondered.

25

A few nights later, after dinner, Sasha and I were sitting on the den couch watching TV. Once again, Sasha was leaning at an impossible angle. Looking back on it, I don't know why it didn't bother me that she didn't fall over.

Maybe because Dad was also holding my hand. We were just so glad to have him around again.

And even though we couldn't see him, it was easy to picture him in his jeans and denim shirt.

Then the den door swung open.

Flump! Sasha instantly fell onto her side.

"You know I don't like you horsing around on the couch," Mom said from the doorway. She must've assumed that Sasha had been bouncing up and down. "And I wish you wouldn't watch so much TV."

"Last show," said Sasha.

"All right." Mom pressed her fingers against her temples. "Funny, a second ago I didn't have a headache."

She closed the den door. Sasha rose up in the air to that crazy angle again as Dad put her back on his lap. I felt that warm sensation close around my hand.

It was starting to feel as if he'd never left.

"Dad, how come you won't let Mom know you're around?" Sasha asked later. We were sitting on the floor of her room, playing Monopoly with him. His properties and money were tucked neatly along one edge of the board.

"Maybe he's worried that she'll totally freak out," I said.

The dice rolled across the board on their own. Then Dad's token, the old shoe, moved to Ventnor Avenue.

"That'll be twelve dollars," I said, taking a ten and two ones from his money.

"But you could prove it to her, Dad," Sasha said. "Just like you proved it to us."

I rolled the dice next and landed on Oriental. Dad owned it with a house. I handed back the twelve bucks plus another sixty-eight.

"Easy come, easy go." I shrugged.

"So how about it, Dad?" Sasha said.

Dad didn't answer, of course.

"Maybe he doesn't want her to know," I said.

"Why not?" Sasha asked as she rolled and moved her token to Water Works.

"I don't know," I said. "Maybe he's worried that she *will* believe it. And then want to stay married and everything. I mean, it's not like they could go out to dinner together."

"They could go to the movies," Sasha said.

The dice rolled across the board by themselves again.

Rap! Rap! Mom knocked on the door and opened it. She looked down at the board and frowned. "Who's the third person?"

"Uh, I'm playing with two pieces," I said.

"And two sets of properties and money?" Mom asked.

"Well, yeah, it's more interesting that way," I said.

"Coach Bosky just called," said Mom. "He wants to know how many seats we'll need at the soccer dinner. Do you want to go, Sasha, or should I get a sitter?"

"What do you do there?" my sister asked.

"We get our championship trophies," I said.

"If I go, can I get a trophy, too?" she asked.

"Get real."

"I'll stay home," Sasha said.

"All right, I'll call Kristen." Mom looked at the Monopoly board again and shook her head wearily as if she couldn't understand us at all.

Briiinnnggg! The phone rang.

"I'll get it." I jumped up and went into Mom's room and closed the door.

"Studying hard?" It was Emily.

"Uh . . ." For a second I forgot what I was supposed to be studying for.

"The math test tomorrow," she said. "You didn't forget, did you?"

"Oh, no way." The truth was I'd let Dad do so much of my math that I was now hopelessly behind. I didn't even bother to pay attention anymore.

"Did you hear about the recital?" she asked.

"No."

"In the gym third period tomorrow, and guess who one of the violin soloists is?"

"Turner?" I'd seen him carrying a violin case to school a few times.

"You got it," Emily said. "I hear he's really good."

"Maybe we can get out of class and go hear him," I said.

"Mars to Kelly," Emily said. "Third period's our math test, remember?"

"Oh, right."

26

I couldn't get the recital out of my head. I didn't quite know why I was so interested in going. I'm not a big fan of classical music. Maybe it wasn't so much that I wanted to see Turner, as I wanted him to see me.

The next day while Ratsky was handing out the test, I raised my hand.

"Yes, Kelly?" he said.

"If we finish the test early, can we go to the recital?" I asked.

"Yes," he replied. "But I doubt you'll have time."

At the start of the test I was determined not to ask Dad for help. But it was filled with problems about ratios and proportions — things that I didn't have a clue about. I looked up at the clock, knowing that if I didn't finish early I'd never get to see Turner.

I looked back down at the test. What was the point? It was hopeless. I'd never be able to finish it anyway.

Dad, could you help? Please?

For a moment nothing happened. Then I felt that resistance.

Oh, come on, Dad, this stuff's too hard. I can't do it.

But the resistance was still there. I could tell he didn't want to do it for me.

I can't believe you'd do this to me. Do you really want me to fail?

Nothing.

All right, then listen. I'll just fill in all the answers wrong and leave. How would you like that?

I felt the resistance waver and then the room seemed to brighten slightly. When I looked down at my test again, everything was filled in.

Ratsky looked surprised when I handed him the test.

"Finished so soon?" he asked.

"Believe it, Mr. Rasky," I said eagerly. "Can I go to the recital?"

"Are you *sure* you don't want to review your answers?" he asked.

"Totally," I said.

"Well, if you're absolutely certain, I guess you can go ahead."

I got to the recital just in time to see Turner walk onto the stage. He was alone, except for the music teacher accompanying him on the piano. He was wearing khaki slacks, a white shirt, and a blue blazer. The auditorium was filled with kids, teachers, and some parents and grandparents. Standing in the back, I couldn't tell if Turner's mom was among them.

Turner and the music teacher began to play. I didn't know much about classical music, but I did know that the sweetly soaring sounds coming from Turner's violin were not an amateur's work. Turner was a serious musician!

When the piece was over, everyone clapped. The parents around me were saying things like, "What an incredible piece!" and "Who is that boy? I've never seen him before."

I wanted to say that he was my friend Turner and that I didn't care if his mother was on TV, but I didn't.

Turner put his violin in its case and came up the aisle. When he saw me, he looked surprised. "Kelly! You listened?"

"You're unreal," I said.

He smiled shyly. "I guess that's what happens when you spend a lot of time by yourself."

I wasn't sure what he meant by that. I looked around for his mom.

"She's not here," he said, as if he could read my mind.

I didn't say anything, but I felt bad for him. If I

played that well, I'd sure want my mom to hear. We left the auditorium and started down the hall.

"She hears me play at home all the time," Turner said, as if he was making excuses for her. "I mean, it's not so bad." We walked a little farther, then he gave me a shy smile. "But I'm kind of glad you came, anyway."

27

"I can't believe how fast you finished the test," Emily said as we walked home together after school that day. "Was it really that easy for you?"

I nodded numbly. What could I say?

"So, did you go to the recital?" she asked.

"Yup."

"Was Turner's mom there?"

I shook my head. "He says she's too busy. But she hears him a lot at home."

"Maybe someday we could talk him into letting us come to the TV station with him," Emily said. "Maybe we could even get on TV."

"Maybe," I said, knowing I'd never ask him to do that.

I was upstairs doing homework when I heard Sasha let herself in. Usually she came upstairs or went into the kitchen for a snack.

But then I heard the front door open and close

again. That was strange. It was cold outside. Where was she going?

I went over to my window and looked out. Down on the street, Sasha rode past on her bike.

Wait a minute! Sasha didn't know how to ride!

I grabbed a jacket and ran outside. Sasha was coming down the street toward me on her bike. I can't say she was actually *riding* it. The bike was wobbling all over the place. Half a dozen times it looked like she should have fallen, but each time the bike magically righted itself.

Magically, that is, unless you knew that Dad was helping her.

I put up my hand to stop her. "What do you think you're doing?"

"I'm learning to ride," Sasha said.

"You can't," I said.

"Why not?"

"What if someone sees you?" I pointed at our neighbors' houses. "Like Jeannette or Mrs. Williamson?"

"So?"

"So, it looks like you're riding all by yourself."

"So?" Sasha still didn't get it.

"So if you really were riding by yourself, you would have fallen ten times already," I said. "People don't start to fall and then all of a sudden *not* fall. Once they start, they fall all the way. If someone sees you they're going to know that something strange is going on."

The corners of my sister's mouth drooped. "I want to learn to ride. It's getting colder and darker every day. If I don't learn now, I'm going to be nine and still not know how."

"Get Mom to teach you," I said.

"She always promises, but she never does," Sasha said.

"You just have to *make* her."

Sasha screwed up her face. "You don't want me to learn. Dad taught you and you don't want him to teach me."

"That's *not* true!" I gasped. "I just don't want everyone to see."

"I don't care who sees!" Sasha fumed. She looked up at the air. "Let's keep trying, Dad."

"No!" I grabbed the handlebars.

Sasha tried to jerk the handlebars away. When that didn't work, she turned her face upward again. "Dad, *please?*"

"Don't do this, Dad," I pleaded. "Someone's bound to see."

"I don't *care!*" Sasha cried.

"You *have* to!" I yelled.

"You're so mean!" Sasha cried. "I hate you!"

"Dad, please don't!" I yelled.

"What in the world is going on?" It was Mom.

28

She was standing by the Dirtmobile. She must've just driven up. Sasha and I were so absorbed in our fight that we hadn't even noticed her.

"Uh, gee, Mom, you're home early." I tried to change the subject.

Mom brushed a loose strand of hair out of her eyes. "Let's go inside, girls."

Sasha left her bike in the driveway and we followed Mom into the house. We sat on the couch in the living room. Mom stood on the other side of the coffee table. Her lips were pressed into a straight line and she looked very serious.

"I'd like to know what that was all about," she said.

"Dad was teaching me to ride," Sasha said. "Then the big slug over here came out and stopped us."

"Dad isn't here, Sasha," Mom said.

"Yes, he is." My sister crossed her arms firmly.

Mom glanced at me.

"He is, Mom," I said. "I know you don't believe us, but it's true."

Mom started to rub her fingers against her temples. "I don't know what to say, girls."

"Just believe us," I said.

"Believe that your father's ghost is here and he was just helping Sasha learn how to ride her bike?" Mom asked.

My sister and I nodded.

"How can you expect me to believe that?" Mom asked.

"Because it's true," Sasha said.

"He straightens our rooms if we ask," I said.

"He cleans the kitchen at night after you leave," Sasha said. "He even does the big slug's homework."

I glared at her. "And *your* Colorado project."

Mom kept rubbing her temples with her fingers. "I'm going upstairs. You'll have to make yourselves something or wait until later for dinner."

She went upstairs.

Sasha and I had made ourselves peanut butter and jelly sandwiches. I guess we could have asked Dad to make us dinner, but we both felt bad and didn't. We were rinsing off the dishes and putting them in the dishwasher when Mom came into the kitchen in her old white bathrobe with the pink stain.

"How come you didn't ask Dad to do the dishes?" she asked.

Neither Sasha nor I answered.

"Is he going to do your homework tonight, Kel?" Mom asked.

I shook my head.

Mom nodded silently as if she understood.

The problem was, she didn't.

29

The next day, Ratsky waited until the end of class to hand back our tests.

"Please stay after class for a moment, Kelly," he said, as he handed me my test. On the top was a big red 100%.

I waited in my seat after the bell rang and the other kids started toward their next class.

"How'd you do?" Emily asked as she passed.

I shyly showed her my test.

"Amazing," she said. "I got an eighty-four. And I've never studied so hard in my life."

She left the room. I waited. When the classroom was empty, Ratsky turned to me.

"That's the best in the class, Kelly," he said, but he didn't look pleased.

"Uh, thanks." I swallowed nervously.

Ratsky flipped a piece of chalk into the air and caught it. I waited, feeling like I was being questioned by the police because I had committed a crime. Well . . . maybe I had.

"I was especially impressed with how easily you did the extra credit work on probabilities," he said. "For instance, that you could figure out so quickly that the chances of a coin turning up heads three times in a row is thirty-three percent."

"Well, I guess it just comes easily to me," I said.

Ratsky nodded and said nothing. I started to feel even more uncomfortable.

"That was the wrong answer, Kelly," he said. "The correct answer is twelve and a half percent. I wonder how you got it right on the test and didn't notice it was wrong just now."

"Well, er . . ." I tried to think of something to say.

Ratsky shook his head. "I'd rather not hear your explanation, Kelly. You may go."

30

The soccer dinner was that night. Kristen came over to sit for Sasha, and Mom drove me to the restaurant where the dinner was held. She was quiet on the way.

"Something wrong, Mom?"

She nodded. "I wasn't going to bring it up until later."

"Bring up what?" I asked.

"I didn't want to ruin the dinner," she said. "I know how excited you are about winning the championship."

My stomach tightened with dread. "What is it, Mom?"

"Mr. Rasky called me at work today," she said.

I slumped down in the car seat and shut my eyes. "You're right. Maybe you should wait until after dinner."

Mom sighed. "A bit late for that now, don't you think?"

I kept my eyes closed and didn't answer.

"How could you know the answer for the test but not know it the next day?" Mom asked.

What could I say?

"Hon?"

"If I told you, you'd never believe it."

Mom glanced at me, the lines in her forehead deepening. "I'm not sure that's an acceptable answer, hon. Now, I'd really like to know."

"You won't believe me."

"You're going to have to do better than that."

"You know what I'm going to say."

Mom stopped at a light and gave me a weary look. "The ghost took the test for you?"

"See?" I said.

"Kelly . . ."

"Then *you* tell me how I did it," I said.

"Did you . . . cheat?"

"How could I cheat if I got a higher grade than everyone else?"

"Maybe you had the answers written down."

"It's math, Mom. Ratsky makes up problems we've never had before. Besides, you have to show your work. You can't just fill in the right answers."

"Then I don't understand," Mom said.

"It won't happen again, Mom. I promise."

I could feel her eyes on me until the car behind us beeped to let her know the light had changed. We started to go. "All right, Kel. I'll accept that."

But my problems that night weren't over.

We got to the restaurant. All the kids in our league were there, and each one had brought at least one of her parents. As usual before dinner began, most of the fathers gathered at the bar while the mothers chatted and the kids ran around.

I found Emily with some of the other girls from the Leopards.

"It's the brain," Emily said.

I wanted to tell her that I wouldn't be getting such good grades anymore. But how do you tell someone that?

"Your dad here?" I asked.

Emily jerked her head toward the bar, where Mr. Davis was holding a drink and laughing with some of the other fathers.

"Time for dinner, everyone," the soccer commissioner—a tall blond man wearing a light brown suit—announced from the podium. We all moved toward our tables. The Leopards had three tables for the team and parents. Mom and I sat with Emily and her dad and Coach Bosky and his daughter, Wendy, and some other girls and their parents.

Soccer dinners were always the same. First we ate, then the league commissioner talked about what a great season it had been and how much he appreciated everyone's participation.

Then the trophies and awards were handed out. The first set of trophies went to the runners-up in the championship. The second set would go to us, the champions. Then came the individual awards for Most Valuable Player, Most Improved Player, and Best Sportsmanship.

The last two awards could be given to any player in the league regardless of her team's record. But the Most Valuable Player award almost always went to someone on the championship team.

"This was some season, huh?" Mr. Davis said to Coach Bosky while we were eating. His face was flushed and his tie was crooked.

"The best I've ever coached," replied Coach Bosky.

"This was your first championship, then?" said Mom.

The coach nodded.

"And just think," said Mr. Davis, "when the season started, you didn't even have a goalie."

"Emily really came through for us," Coach Bosky said.

"Well, of course," Mr. Davis said with a smile. "She had a great instructor."

Coach Bosky and Mom laughed because, of course, Emily's instructor was her father. But Emily blushed and squirmed a little in her seat.

"Dad, don't brag," she said.

"Hey, come on, sweetheart, I was only kidding," Mr. Davis said. Then he turned to Coach Bosky. "But you have to admit, she made herself into one heck of a goalie."

"Dad, stop it!" Emily's face grew redder.

"But it's true," her father said. "There's no way this team could've won the championship without you." He turned to Coach Bosky again. "I'm telling you, Coach, I never saw a kid work so hard to rise to the occasion as Emily did."

This time Coach Bosky just nodded. Maybe Emily was right. Maybe her dad was bragging.

We got our championship trophies and then the soccer commissioner started on the individual awards. The Best Sportsmanship award went to a girl on another team.

"This next award is for most improved player," the commissioner said, lifting the gold statuette. Emily's eyes were locked on it and her mouth hung slightly open. She probably wasn't even aware that her hands were clasped tightly together as if she was praying.

Her father stopped swirling the ice in his glass and

didn't move. You could see how much Emily wanted that award, and how much her father thought she deserved it.

"Becky Sinclair of the Tigers," the soccer commissioner announced.

A whoop and a cheer went up from the Tigers' table, and a beaming, red-faced girl with a wide smile jumped up and went to collect her trophy. At our table, Emily's shoulders slumped. Next to her, Mr. Davis narrowed his eyes, swirled his drink, and gulped it down.

"That's all right, sweetheart," he said. "It just means that you must be getting the Most Valuable Player award." As he said that, he leveled his gaze at Coach Bosky. "They just don't want to overload one team with too many trophies, right, Coach?"

Coach Bosky didn't respond. Since the coaches got together to choose whom the individual awards went to, he already knew who was getting it.

"And that brings us to the award for league MVP," the soccer commissioner announced, lifting the last trophy. "The award for the most valuable player goes to . . . Kelly Halkit."

31

M*e?* I couldn't believe it!

"Oh, hon! That's fantastic! Congratulations!" Mom hugged me.

Everyone at the Leopards' tables stood up and started to clap. Everyone, that is, except Emily and her father. Emily stared down at the table, looking crushed. Her father gazed away, his lips pressed together in a hard, unyielding line.

I felt someone nudge me and turned to find Coach Bosky smiling. "Go on, Kelly," he said. "Go get it. You deserve it."

I looked at Emily again. This time our eyes met. Hers glistened and threatened to spill over with tears, but she forced a crooked smile onto her lips and nodded as if she was trying her best to be happy for me.

And then I went to get the award . . . that I didn't deserve.

*   *   *

The soccer dinner always ended with a raffle of things like soccer balls, free video rentals, and a free week at the town soccer camp at the end of the summer. I sat through it in a daze. The MVP trophy stood on the table before me. Near the bottom was a small brass plate. Engraved on it was:

Most Valuable Player
Kelly Halkit

Reminding me of what a fake I was.

Mr. Davis stared down at his empty glass with a stony look. Emily tried to get interested in the raffle, but at least twice I saw her peek at the trophy with a hurt expression on her face.

The whole thing was so wrong.

"What is it, hon?" Mom whispered in my ear.

"I don't deserve this," I whispered back.

"Hon, everyone feels that way," Mom tried to reassure me. "But you do deserve it. They wouldn't have given it to you if you didn't."

"They didn't know," I whispered.

"Didn't know what?" Mom asked.

I just shook my head. How could I explain?

The raffle ended, and with it, the dinner. Mr. Davis heaved himself up out of his chair. "Come on, Emily, let's go."

He sounded bitter and angry. Emily started to get

up, and as she did, our eyes met again. This was my best friend.

"Wait!" I suddenly blurted. I turned to Coach Bosky. "Is there any way you can give this to Emily?" I picked up the Most Valuable Player trophy. "She's the one who really deserves it."

Coach Bosky frowned. "I'm sorry, Kelly. That's a very nice gesture, but the decision's been made."

"But she really does deserve it," I insisted. "More than me. We didn't even have a goalie at the beginning of year. Remember that save she made in the championship game? Without it, we wouldn't have won."

"Emily was great," Coach Bosky said. "But the award is for you."

"I agree with the coach, Kelly." Mr. Davis butted in. "You deserve to be MVP." Then he turned to Coach Bosky. "But with all due respect, sir, I can't understand how my daughter could go from never having played goalie before in her life to being the goalie for the championship team and not be named Most *Improved* Player."

Coach Bosky stiffened. "The decision was made by all the coaches, Mr. Davis," he replied in an icy tone. "If you'd like to have a say, perhaps you should volunteer to be a coach *next* year."

"I really think we'd better go, Dad." Emily tugged anxiously at her father's arm.

Mr. Davis let himself be coaxed a few steps away, but then changed his mind and stepped back to Coach Bosky again. I held my breath. It looked as if Mr. Davis and Coach Bosky were going to have a fight.

32

But just when I expected Mr. Davis to say something angry or nasty, he shoved his hands into his pockets. "Listen, Coach, I think you did a tremendous job with these kids this year. I could never have done what you did. But I also think deep down even you know my daughter deserved Most Improved Player."

Emily pulled at her father's arm again. "It's not that important, Dad. Let's just go."

But Mr. Davis wouldn't budge. He was waiting for Coach Bosky's reply.

"Well, Mr. Davis, I will tell you this," Coach Bosky said. "We only give three individual awards each year and we have an understanding among the coaches that no team should collect more than one."

"And the MVP award always goes to a player on the championship team," Mr. Davis said.

"That's correct," replied Coach Bosky.

"So even if Emily deserved Most Improved, she couldn't get it," Mr. Davis surmised.

Coach Bosky hung his head slightly. "We do the best we can. I'm truly sorry Emily didn't receive more recognition."

Mr. Davis smiled proudly and put his arm around Emily's shoulder. "You hear that, sweetheart?"

He was so proud of her. The only reason he'd argued and been obnoxious was because he loved her.

Suddenly I had an idea. "Then why can't Emily and I share the MVP award?"

"You don't have to," Mr. Davis said. "I just wanted Emily to know that she deserved Most Improved even if she didn't get it."

"But she deserves this, too," I said, nodding at the Most Valuable Player trophy. "I'm not just saying it. She really does."

"It's okay, Kel," Emily said. "You take it."

"No, Em, I really mean it," I said. "I wouldn't have gotten this if it wasn't for you." I turned to Coach Bosky. "Isn't there anything you can do?"

Coach Bosky ran his fingers through his white hair. "Wait here a second." He left us and walked over to the soccer commissioner, who was standing near the podium talking to some people. We watched as our coach took the commissioner aside and spoke quietly in his ear. Finally the commissioner nodded. Coach Bosky came back toward us.

"If you'd like, we'll have both of your names engraved on it," he said.

"Great!" I eagerly handed the trophy back to him.

"Are you sure?" Emily gasped.

"Totally," I said.

"Oh, Kelly!" Emily threw her arms around my neck and hugged me. If only she knew how much better it made me feel.

33

"That was a very admirable thing you did," Mom said as we drove home.

"Thanks."

"I'm just curious. Did you do it because Emily is your best friend, or because you really think that she deserves it?"

"More than I do, Mom."

"I don't know how you can say that. All the coaches picked you."

"I know." She didn't want to hear about ghosts. "Hon?"

"It's okay, Mom. It's much better this way."

We pulled into our driveway. It seemed like every light in the house was burning brightly.

"I wish they'd learn to turn off the lights," Mom muttered as we went up the steps. We paused at the front door while she searched for her keys. Suddenly the door swung open and Kristen bounded past us and down the steps.

"Kristen? Wait! Is something wrong?" Mom called behind her. "I didn't pay you. Kristen?"

Kristen disappeared down the sidewalk and into the dark. With a bewildered look on her face, Mom stepped into the house. Sasha was standing by the light switch in the living room.

"What happened with Kristen?" Mom asked. "Why are all the lights on?"

"Kristen turned them on," Sasha said and switched the light off.

"Why?" Mom asked.

"Because I told her about Dad."

Mom scowled, then pressed her fingers against her temples. "You . . . oh, no, not that he's a ghost."

Sasha nodded and walked to the floor lamp on the other side of the room. She turned that off, too. The living room started to get darker.

"Oh, for Pete's sake, Sasha." Mom started to get aggravated. "You must have scared the daylights out of her. Now what am I going to do about a baby-sit —"

She didn't finish the sentence. Sasha had just turned off another light, making the living room dark. Mom's jaw dropped and her hands slowly fell away from her forehead.

A dull glow filled the room.

"What is it?" Mom asked.

"Dad," Sasha replied. "From now on he can baby-sit."

"Ready?" Sasha asked. We were sitting at the kitchen table, holding Mom's hands. Not because it was a séance, but just to keep her calm.

Mom nodded slowly. She was trembling. "As ready as I'll ever be."

We'd just spent twenty minutes telling her the story all over again. Now the Monopoly game made sense to her, and we even confessed that Dad had probably been involved in messing up her dates with Mr. Stark.

At first she'd thought the glowing was some kind of a trick and had searched the living room for the source of the light. She only gave up when we made the den glow, and then the kitchen.

"You decide where he should go next," Sasha said.

"Umm . . . the living room again," Mom said.

Through the kitchen doorway, we saw the living room glow.

"Now here in the kitchen again," she said.

The glow surrounded us.

"Believe us now?" Sasha asked.

Instead of answering, Mom turned toward the dark kitchen window. "The tree house."

Out in the backyard, the glow seeped out from between the wooden boards of the tree house.

Mom's grip on my hand tightened. "I don't believe this," she whispered.

"Easy, Mom," I groaned. If she squeezed any harder she was going to break my fingers.

"Dad, should Mom be scared or anything?" Sasha asked.

The glow filtered into the kitchen again. It felt so soft and warm that you just knew it wasn't bad.

"And it's really you, Dad, right?" Sasha said.

The glow flickered gently.

"But how?" Mom's voice was a hoarse whisper.

The kitchen grew dark for a moment, then the glow returned.

"He doesn't know, Mom," I translated.

"But you're really here?" Mom asked the glow.

Once again, the kitchen flickered.

Mom pressed her hands to her face and started to cry.

Sasha and I stayed up late. Mom had gone into her room and didn't come out. We could see the glow coming from under her door. Despite everything that had happened, my little sister still wanted me to read her a story. I read her a funny story about a boy who switches bodies with a dog. No ghost stories that night.

34

"Kids, get up! You're late!"

My eyelids felt heavy. It took a big effort just to open them.

"You're going to miss your bus if you don't get up right now!"

I dragged myself out of bed and pulled on some clothes. As I stumbled out of my room, I heard nothing from Sasha's room. I doubted she was even awake.

I knocked on her door. "Come on, Sasha, we're late."

No answer. Well, that was her problem.

Down in the kitchen I slid into my seat. The curtains were drawn and the lights were off, but it was sunny outside and the light still crept in. It was hard to tell if Dad was there. I sat still for a moment . . . yes, he was there. I could feel him.

On the other side of the kitchen counter, Mom took a sip of coffee. She was wearing her bathrobe.

Usually she'd be hurrying back upstairs to get dressed and do her hair.

"Aren't you going to work today?" I asked.

She shook her head. "I'm staying home."

"Can I stay home, too?" I asked.

"No, you have to go to school."

"No fair," I complained.

"Yes, it is," Mom said. "You've known about him for weeks. This is my first day. Where's Sasha?"

"In bed, where else?" I said.

"Oh, for —" Mom caught herself. "Hon, do you think you could help?"

"Give me a break, Mom, I just got down here," I complained.

"I didn't mean you, Kel," Mom replied.

"Oh."

The kitchen became slightly cooler and darker.

Crash! I jumped at the sound of something crashing to the floor. Mom had put her coffee mug down on the edge of the counter and it had fallen off.

"Sorry, hon. This is going to take some getting used to," she said with a crooked smile. She grabbed a dish towel and bent down to mop up the coffee.

It wasn't long before Sasha trudged into the kitchen with her hair in a rat's nest. Her hairbrush, shoes, and socks were under her arm. Once again the kitchen grew warmer and brighter. Sasha sat down and dumped her stuff on the chair next to her. She propped her chin on her hands and stared grumpily into space.

"You don't have much time," Mom said. "You're not even dressed and your hair's a mess."

"I can't eat unless my shoes and socks are on," Sasha replied.

"Then put them on," I said.

"I need help," she said.

"Give me a break," I groaned.

Sasha looked up in the air. "Dad, put my shoes and socks on."

I ducked my head under the table, expecting to see a sock slide up each of her feet, followed by her shoes.

But nothing happened.

"Come on, Dad," Sasha said impatiently.

Still nothing.

"Maybe he's not going to do it," I said.

Little furrows appeared in my sister's forehead. "Why not?"

"Maybe he thinks you should do it yourself," I said.

"He does everything else," Sasha complained. "He helped get me up this morning."

"Maybe Mom really needed that help," I said. "Maybe you really don't."

Sasha wrinkled her nose. "How do *you* know what he thinks, smarty-pants?"

I told her how lately every time I asked Dad to do something for me I felt that weird resistance, like he didn't want to do it. And how it reminded me of all the times when he'd done stuff for us, but then said we had to learn to do it ourselves.

Sasha crossed her arms. "Well, I'm not putting my shoes and socks on. So if Dad won't help, I guess I just won't go to school today. Hear that, Dad?"

The light in the kitchen flickered and one of Sasha's white socks actually started to rise off the chair.

"Don't, Dad," I said.

The sock fell limply to the chair.

"I can't be seeing this," Mom muttered.

"Yes, Dad, do it!" Sasha said.

"Don't, Dad, really," I said. "This can't be what you want. You always said you wanted us to learn to take care of ourselves. I know you love us and want to do things for us, but do you really want us to get As on tests when we don't know the math?"

"What?" Mom gasped.

"Don't listen to her, Dad," Sasha said. "She just wants to keep you all to herself."

Meanwhile, Mom stared at me. "That math test

Mr. Rasky called me about. The one you did so well on."

I slumped down in the seat. "I told you it wouldn't happen again."

"All those times you said you'd finished your homework in school and then watched TV all night," Mom said. "Oh, Kelly, that's terrible."

"He only helped me with math. I swear." I looked across the kitchen table at Sasha, who stuck her tongue out.

"Are you sure?" Mom asked. "Is there anything else you haven't told me about?"

"Sasha tried to get him to teach her to ride her bike," I said.

"Boy-oh-boy." Sasha laughed disdainfully. "*That's* a big crime."

"We weren't talking about Sasha," Mom said. "We were talking about you."

"That's all," I said.

"How about soccer?" Sasha asked.

"Shut up!" I yelled at her.

Mom blinked. "Oh, no, not the MVP award."

What could I say?

"No wonder," Mom said to herself. She gazed out the kitchen window at the tree house for a moment. Then she looked up at the kitchen clock. "I'm driving you to school today. Finish eating, straighten up the kitchen, and see if you can get to your rooms."

She started out of the kitchen.

Sasha and I shared a look.

Mom suddenly stopped. "I take that back. *Don't* straighten the kitchen or your rooms. Don't do anything that involves Dad until I have more time to think about this."

35

"When it comes back from the en-graver," Emily said at lunch that day, "you should get the trophy first."

"You take it," I said.

"But it's not right," Emily said. "You're the one they awarded it to."

"I want you to have it," I said. The truth was, I didn't feel right taking it. I didn't know if I'd *ever* feel right about it.

Scott put his lunch tray down on the table and joined us. "Salutations, babes."

"So where's Turner?" Emily asked, putting into words what I was thinking.

"Country Day Academy," Scott answered.

Emily and I gave each other shocked looks. Then I said, "I thought he wasn't going there until after Christmas."

"It's just a tryout," he said. "They have kids come for a day or two. To get a feel for the place."

"Oh well." Emily acted like she didn't care.

But I did. I didn't want Turner to go. *Dad, do you think you could —*

I caught myself. I was just about to ask Dad to make sure Turner had a terrible day so that he'd decide to come back to our school. But I knew it was wrong.

"I'll be sorry when he really goes," Scott said. "He's a pretty cool guy, no matter who his mother is."

I nodded dumbly and felt sort of depressed. I wasn't just sorry to see Turner go; I hated the thought.

Scott and Emily chattered about other things after that, but I couldn't stop thinking about Turner. Could I ask Dad for one last wish? And then swear never to use him again, ever?

No, I couldn't do it.

Scott finished his lunch and went to the gym to shoot baskets until the period ended.

"So, what do you think?" Emily asked after he left.

"About what?" I asked.

"You know what I'm talking about," she said. "Are you unhappy?"

"I don't know."

"I thought you liked him more than that," she said.

I smiled at her. "I thought *you* liked him more than that."

"He's too short." She winked.

"What about his mom and the wire wheels?" I asked.

"They don't make him any taller." Emily grinned. "But you're the one who really likes him. Admit it."

What was the sense in denying it? "Okay, I admit it."

"Maybe you could get him to change his mind," she said.

If she only knew how easy it would be.

"Dream on, Em."

36

The first thing I noticed when I got home that afternoon was that the Dirtmobile was gone. In its place stood the same old car, but it was clean and shiny. I went into the house. The carpet was vacuumed and everything was neat and straightened up. And there was a funny smell in the air — like bread baking.

"That you, Kel?" Mom stepped out of the kitchen. She was wearing jeans and a white sweatshirt. Her hair was in a French braid.

"Yeah," I said. "The car looks great."

"I had it washed," Mom said. "And I had the oil changed and the tires checked."

I went into the kitchen and looked around. It was spotless. Even the faucet was fixed. "Looks like you and Dad have been busy."

"Just me, hon," Mom said.

"What about the drip?"

"Well." Mom smiled. "Me *and* the plumber."

"How come?"

"Because you're right," she said. "What Dad always wanted was for us to take care of ourselves. So how would you like to help me make a stew?"

"Why?"

"So that we can have it for dinner tonight, and save the leftovers for nights when I don't have time to cook," she said.

"Like instead of having frozen dinners?" I asked.

"Yes," Mom said. "Exactly."

I was peeling potatoes and carrots when Sasha got home.

"What's the story?" she asked as she came into the kitchen. She was wearing her pink parka with the white fur trim.

"We're cooking," I said.

"Wow!" She looked around in amazement and started to unzip her jacket.

"Don't take it off, hon." Mom dried her hands with a dish towel.

"Why not?"

"Because we're going outside," Mom said. "It's time you learned how to ride a bike."

37

"Time to get up, Kel." The next morning I woke to find Mom sitting at the side of my bed, stroking my hair. The sun was just starting to come up, and I could hear birds singing outside. I stretched and yawned, then noticed the clock.

"It's early, Mom."

She nodded. "From now on we're all getting up early. No more last-minute panics."

She was already dressed for work and her hair was brushed and in a ponytail. A sweet, yummy smell was in the air.

"What's that?" I asked.

"Pancakes," she said, standing up. "Get dressed. I'll wake Sasha and we'll all have breakfast together."

When I got downstairs the kitchen table was set with plates, glasses, and silverware. A pitcher of orange juice and a milk carton stood next to a platter with a mound of steaming pancakes on it.

It smelled great.

I was halfway through my pancakes when Mom and Sasha came in. My sister was in one of her bad moods.

"Tie my shoes?" she asked.

"No way," I replied.

"I can't eat until my shoes are tied," she said.

"Then you're going to be hungry," said Mom.

"I can't go to school, either," said Sasha.

"Then you're going to spend a lonely day at home," Mom said.

Sasha slouched down in her chair, tucked her chin against her chest, and didn't budge.

She still hadn't moved when I left the kitchen and went back upstairs to make my bed. A little while later I heard her come upstairs. From the sound of her footsteps, I could tell she'd put her shoes on.

Bang! Sasha slammed the door to her room. By then I'd finished making my bed. As I went out to the top of the stairs, I heard her in her room.

"Dad, please, I don't have time."

I stepped toward the door and raised my hand to knock.

"Don't, Kelly."

I whirled around. Mom was standing behind me.

"But —" I began.

Mom pressed a finger to her lips and shook her head.

Then I heard Sasha say, *"Oh, come on, Dad, why not?"*

Mom motioned for me to follow her downstairs and out to the car. It wasn't long before Sasha came out and got into the backseat. The corners of her mouth were turned down and she had a sour look on her face.

Mom looked at her in the rearview mirror. "Room straightened and bed made?"

Sasha stared out the window and didn't answer.

38

I wasn't certain how long Mom would keep it up, but every morning she made us breakfast, and only once did we have frozen microwaved dinners at night. She expanded the star chart to include setting the table, doing dishes, sweeping, and vacuuming.

It was time for our next big math test. When Ratsky handed the tests back, mine didn't have a grade on it. But in the top right corner he'd written in red ink, "Please see me after class."

I waited until everyone else left. Ratsky sat behind his desk and motioned for me to sit in the wooden chair beside it.

"This is starting to become a habit," he said.

"Sorry?"

"Asking you to stay after class," he said. "Do you know why you're here?"

"I bombed the test, right?"

Ratsky nodded. "You've gone from best to worst in the class. I wish I understood it."

I stared down at my hands and didn't answer. Talk about things coming back to haunt you.

"You think it's funny?" Mr. Ratsky asked, surprised.

"Oh, no." I realized I'd smiled. "I . . . I'm totally lost in class."

"Do you think you can catch up?" he asked. "Is there anyone at home who could help you?"

There was . . .

But not anymore. I shook my head. "Maybe I should move to an easier class."

Ratsky sat back in his chair. "If you really feel that way, I'll have to meet with the rest of the staff. I expect they'll agree."

I can't say I was thrilled, but I knew I deserved it.

Emily and I caught up to each other at lunch, and I told her what had happened.

"You have to go into remedial math because you failed *one* test?" she asked in disbelief.

"Believe me," I said, "it's the best thing."

She rolled her eyes. "If you say so. Anyway, you ready to take the trophy yet? I've had it for a week already."

"Why don't you keep it a little longer," I said.

39

I was doing my homework that afternoon when I heard Sasha let herself into the house. She came upstairs but didn't go into her room. She went into Mom's.

She stayed in there for a long time. Finally I got up and went to see what she was doing.

I opened the door. Mom's bedroom was dim and empty. I went to Dad's closet and opened it. Sasha was sitting on the floor hugging Puffy. Dad's briefcase was next to her, and she was holding his wallet close to her nose.

It was dark in the closet and hard to see anything more than her outline. But I had the feeling she'd been crying. I sat down.

"Why'd you and Mom have to make him go away?" she asked with a sniff.

"How do you know he went away?" I asked.

"Because he doesn't do anything anymore." She wiped her eyes with the palm of her hand.

"Maybe he doesn't want to."

Sasha shook her head as if she didn't believe that. "He always did before."

"Remember what he used to say every time he did something for us?" I asked. "That someday we'd have to learn to do it ourselves."

"Other kids don't," she said.

"Sure they do."

"I don't want him to go!" Sasha sobbed and pressed her hands to her face. I crawled over and hugged her. She trembled and sniffed. It made me want to cry, too, but I tried to be strong. I knew I had to help Sasha grow up. She was just a little kid.

Later that evening I was setting the kitchen table. It had started to snow outside, and the yard and trees were covered with a fine blanket of white. Mom was heating up the meat loaf we'd made earlier in the week. We'd already had it twice, but it was still better than microwaved food every night.

"You know, I haven't had a single headache since the soccer dinner," Mom said, as she made a salad.

"Why do you think?" I asked.

"I think I knew that Dad was trying to reach me all that time," Mom said. "Of course, I couldn't accept the idea. I wouldn't let myself believe that it was possible. I thought it was just my imagination playing tricks on me. I concentrated so hard on *not* believing that it gave me headaches."

I told her about Sasha in Dad's closet that afternoon.

Mom nodded and looked out at the tree house. We could see it outlined in white.

"I used to think that heaven was all white and still, like the world after a snowfall," she said. "I wonder if your father brought a little bit of heaven to us."

"How?" I asked.

"Maybe what happened to us is a very special thing," she said. "I don't know why or how it happened. . . . Maybe it doesn't even matter. What matters is that we didn't lose Dad after all. In some way he's still here."

"But if he's still here, then why isn't he *here*?" Sasha asked. She was standing in the kitchen doorway. Her eyes were still red and her cheeks were streaked with the salty trail of dried tears.

"I don't know that he's not here," Mom said. "He just isn't doing what he did before. He knows that you girls have to keep growing and learning. You have to become self-sufficient. Me, too. Having Dad tie your shoes and make your bed isn't good for you, Sasha. Just like it isn't good for your sister to use him for homework and to win soccer games."

"What if we promise *never* to use him for those things again?" Sasha asked.

"That's the problem," Mom said. "We all want to think we won't use him. But in a moment of weakness, when there's something we really, really want, and there's no other way to get it, we will. And that's no good, because one of the most important lessons we have to learn in life is that we can't have everything we want. We have to settle for a few things, and even those may take a lot of work to get."

"You're not going to make him go away, are you?" Sasha asked.

Mom was quiet for a moment. A tear formed in her eye and she rubbed it away. "It's not up to me, hon. I love your father, and I will love him for a long, long time."

Sasha started to sob again. Mom kneeled down and took her into her arms. She looked over Sasha's shoulder at me. "You too, Kel?"

I joined them for a three-way hug.

"From now on the three of us are going to be a team," Mom said. "We're going to be everything Dad wanted us to be. As long as we do that, he'll always be with us."

It may have been my imagination, but I could swear the kitchen brightened for a moment.

40

It was the week after Christmas vacation. I was in an easier math class now, but my new teacher said that if I worked really hard I would probably be able to go back to Ratsky's class by the end of March.

Turner had called a few nights before and we'd talked for a long time about his skiing trip and his new school. He asked if I'd like to come to his mom's TV studio over the weekend and watch her record a segment on hip fractures. I said I'd love to.

We were still getting up early every morning and eating breakfast together. On Sunday afternoons we cooked a big meal with lots of leftovers for the rest of the week. I wish I could say that we managed to keep our rooms neat and make our beds every day, but hey, no one's perfect. Still, we did keep the house neater than before.

And even though Sasha didn't earn anything near 200 stars, she got Andy Panda for Christmas.

And I wasn't too jealous.

The last thing Dad said before he went away was, "Nothing bad is going to happen."

For a while I was really mad at him for breaking his promise. Then I realized he didn't know. He *couldn't* have known. He'd only said it to make me feel better.

It was just another way of saying, "I love you."

About the Author

Todd Strasser has written many award-winning novels for young and teenage readers. Among his best-known books are *Help! I'm Trapped in Obedience School* and *Girl Gives Birth to Own Prom Date*. He speaks frequently at schools about the craft of writing and conducts writing workshops for young people. He and his family live in Westchester, New York, with their yellow Labrador retriever, Mac.